Tinhorn's Daughter

L. RON HUBBARD

Tinhorn's Daughter

GALAXY PRESS

Published by
Galaxy Press, LLC
7051 Hollywood Boulevard, Suite 200
Hollywood, CA 90028

Printed in the United States of America.

ISBN-10 1-59212-372-4
ISBN-13 978-1-59212-372-8

Library of Congress Control Number: 2007928448

Contents

Stories from Pulp Fiction's Golden Age

A ND it *was* a golden age.

The 1930s and 1940s were a vibrant, seminal time for a gigantic audience of eager readers, probably the largest per capita audience of readers in American history. The magazine racks were chock-full of publications with ragged trims, garish cover art, cheap brown pulp paper, low cover prices—and the most excitement you could hold in your hands.

"Pulp" magazines, named for their rough-cut, pulpwood paper, were a vehicle for more amazing tales than Scheherazade could have told in a million and one nights. Set apart from higher-class "slick" magazines, printed on fancy glossy paper with quality artwork and superior production values, the pulps were for the "rest of us," adventure story after adventure story for people who liked to *read*. Pulp fiction authors were no-holds-barred entertainers—real storytellers. They were more interested in a thrilling plot twist, a horrific villain or a white-knuckle adventure than they were in lavish prose or convoluted metaphors.

The sheer volume of tales released during this wondrous golden age remains unmatched in any other period of literary history—hundreds of thousands of published stories in over nine hundred different magazines. Some titles lasted only an issue or two; many magazines succumbed to paper shortages during World War II, while others endured for decades yet. Pulp fiction remains as a treasure trove of stories you can read, stories you can love, stories you can remember. The stories were driven by plot and character, with grand heroes, terrible villains, beautiful damsels (often in distress), diabolical plots, amazing places, breathless romances. The readers wanted to be taken beyond the mundane, to live adventures far removed from their ordinary lives—and the pulps rarely failed to deliver.

In that regard, pulp fiction stands in the tradition of all memorable literature. For as history has shown, good stories are much more than fancy prose. William Shakespeare, Charles Dickens, Jules Verne, Alexandre Dumas—many of the greatest literary figures wrote their fiction for the readers, not simply literary colleagues and academic admirers. And writers for pulp magazines were no exception. These publications reached an audience that dwarfed the circulations of today's short story magazines. Issues of the pulps were scooped up and read by over thirty million avid readers each month.

Because pulp fiction writers were often paid no more than a cent a word, they had to become prolific or starve. They also had to write aggressively. As Richard Kyle, publisher and editor of *Argosy*, the first and most long-lived of the pulps, so pointedly explained: "The pulp magazine writers, the best of them, worked for markets that did not write for critics or attempt to satisfy timid advertisers. Not having to answer to anyone other than their readers, they wrote about human beings on the edges of the unknown, in those new lands the future would explore. They wrote for what we would become, not for what we had already been."

Some of the more lasting names that graced the pulps include H. P. Lovecraft, Edgar Rice Burroughs, Robert E. Howard, Max Brand, Louis L'Amour, Elmore Leonard, Dashiell Hammett, Raymond Chandler, Erle Stanley Gardner, John D. MacDonald, Ray Bradbury, Isaac Asimov, Robert Heinlein—and, of course, L. Ron Hubbard.

In a word, he was among the most prolific and popular writers of the era. He was also the most enduring—hence this series—and certainly among the most legendary. It all began only months after he first tried his hand at fiction, with L. Ron Hubbard tales appearing in *Thrilling Adventures, Argosy, Five-Novels Monthly, Detective Fiction Weekly, Top-Notch, Texas Ranger, War Birds, Western Stories,* even *Romantic Range.* He could write on any subject, in any genre, from jungle explorers to deep-sea divers, from G-men and gangsters, cowboys and flying aces to mountain climbers, hard-boiled detectives and spies. But he really began to shine when he turned his talent to science fiction and fantasy of which he authored nearly fifty novels or novelettes to forever change the shape of those genres.

Following in the tradition of such famed authors as Herman Melville, Mark Twain, Jack London and Ernest Hemingway, Ron Hubbard actually lived adventures that his own characters would have admired—as an ethnologist among primitive tribes, as prospector and engineer in hostile climes, as a captain of vessels on four oceans. He even wrote a series of articles for *Argosy,* called "Hell Job," in which he lived and told of the most dangerous professions a man could put his hand to.

Finally, and just for good measure, he was also an accomplished photographer, artist, filmmaker, musician and educator. But he was first and foremost a *writer,* and that's the L. Ron Hubbard we come to know through the pages of this volume.

This library of Stories from the Golden Age presents the best of L. Ron Hubbard's fiction from the heyday of storytelling, the Golden Age of the pulp magazines. In these eighty volumes, readers are treated to a full banquet of 153 stories, a kaleidoscope of tales representing every imaginable genre: science fiction, fantasy, western, mystery, thriller, horror, even romance—action of all kinds and in all places.

Because the pulps themselves were printed on such inexpensive paper with high acid content, issues were not meant to endure. As the years go by, the original issues of every pulp from *Argosy* through *Zeppelin Stories* continue crumbling into brittle, brown dust. This library preserves the L. Ron Hubbard tales from that era, presented with a distinctive look that brings back the nostalgic flavor of those times.

L. Ron Hubbard's Stories from the Golden Age has something for every taste, every reader. These tales will return you to a time when fiction was good clean entertainment and the most fun a kid could have on a rainy afternoon or the best thing an adult could enjoy after a long day at work.

Pick up a volume, and remember what reading is supposed to be all about. Remember curling up with a *great story.*

—Kevin J. Anderson

KEVIN J. ANDERSON *is the author of more than ninety critically acclaimed works of speculative fiction, including The Saga of Seven Suns, the continuation of the Dune Chronicles with Brian Herbert, and his* New York Times *bestselling novelization of L. Ron Hubbard's* Ai! Pedrito!

Tinhorn's Daughter

CHAPTER ONE

Kidnapped

EARLY that morning, when they had left the stage station, Betsy Trotwood had supposed that they would reach the clearly outlined Rockies by midmorning.

But at noon, the Rockies were just as far westward, apparently, as they had been at the start. And even now, with dusk coming on, the rolling Concord stage and its six chunky horses were just entering the foothills of the higher peaks beyond.

In truth, Montana was an amazing country, especially to a girl outside the city limits of Boston for the first time in her life. The land was so BIG, so lacking in people, so empty of women!

The Concord's rumble and creak made small headway against the silent immensities and Betsy Trotwood thought that if she had to sit silent and alone much longer she would go mad.

The stage rolled into Twin Pines and the resulting commotion spared her sanity. Red-faced men in big hats, all dressed in stained leather, each one burdened with an enormous revolver and belt, gathered around the pausing stage for news.

The log stage station, scarred by arrows and bullets, looked very isolated, backed by the rearing foothills and dwarfed by the skyward rearing pines.

Red-faced men in big hats, all dressed in stained leather, each one burdened with an enormous revolver and belt, gathered around the pausing stage for news.

The half-dozen men had approached with loud, coarse shouts addressed to the messenger and driver, but Bat had scowled and jerked his thumb down and the crowd had instantly removed hats, shuffled, peered and had begun to walk around on tiptoe. They still wanted news but they asked for it in whispers.

Betsy Trotwood knew that she was the cause of this sensation but she could not understand it. They acted as though she were dead and on her way to a funeral.

Her appearance belied anything like that. Her voluminous skirts were patterned in gay little flowers and her ripply brimmed hat was tied under her chin with a bright blue ribbon.

Bat Connor, the messenger, climbed down from the box and went inside. He came back a moment later swiping his hairy hand across his bleached whiskers and looking guiltily toward Betsy to see if she had noticed anything wrong.

Horses were being changed as this last run from Twin Pines to Puma Pass would be completed before midnight, and while Tom, the sober-faced driver, tried to remember to swear under his breath as the horses were changed, Bat took advantage of the pause to shift his Winchester into the crook of his arm, put his boot on the step and converse with the passenger. He wanted the boys to see the intimate terms he was on with her.

"Ridin' easy, miss?" said Bat, spraying a hub of tobacco juice.

"It is a little rough," ventured Betsy.

"Won't be no more stage when the railroad gets through here and across the Rockies," volunteered Bat. "Steel's better ridin', I guess, but it shore looks like the country is gettin' all settled up. You goin' as far as Puma Pass, ain't you, ma'am?"

"Yes, if my father is there," said Betsy.

Bat turned to the crowd. "Slim Trotwood still in Puma Pass, boys?"

The group looked thunderstruck for an instant and then brightly nodded all together.

"He's still in Puma Pass," relayed Bat. "And we'll git you there. Just you wait and see. Ain't a road agent could ever get up nerve enough to hold up any stage of mine!"

"Road agent?" said Betsy, startled.

"Shore," said Bat. "We call 'em road agents because they stops us where they ain't no station, see? Bandits."

"You mean there are robbers in these hills?"

Bat grinned confidently and patted his Winchester as though it were a cat. "Now don't worry none about it, ma'am. You got me ridin' the box."

The station boss felt a little jealous of Bat's intimacy. He growled, "Sunset Maloney wasn't scared none the *last* time."

"You've been held up?" said Betsy quickly.

The crowd was instantly all compassion again. She looked very small and very pretty and just now, scared.

"Aw, it ain't often," said the station boss.

"But you *have* been held up," she insisted to Bat.

He looked uncomfortable and gnawed a chunk from a villainous black plug before he answered. "Well, yes. A young feller named Sunset Maloney's been holdin' up stages every time they's a money sack goin' in to your old man."

"He's been stealing from my father?"

"Sure. Slim Trotwood, as agent for the Great Western Railroad, is always havin' a wad shipped in to him. In fact, we're carryin' one right now."

Bat saw glory in his role. "Last time I put up a rarin' fight and this time he won't have nerve enough to come within six miles of the stage. You just trust to me, ma'am."

"What sort of fellow is this Sunset Maloney?" said Betsy.

"Pretty wild," replied Bat judicially. "Pretty wild. Faster'n a greased rattler with a six-gun. He's ornery as a barrel of wildcats. But we won't have no trouble."

Tom was hitched up again and Bat dragged himself back to the box, Winchester prominently displayed. The half-dozen station men tipped their hats to Miss Trotwood and the Concord rolled on its dusty way again.

The horses labored as they pulled the long grade. The road began to wind around high hills, and far below, Betsy could see winding streams all silver with distance. The world was turning scarlet and gold as the sun dipped behind the backbone of the continent. But none of this warm beauty lightened Betsy's heart.

She felt very small and helpless, shaken like a die in the otherwise empty coach. And now she had a new worry. Her father was losing his money to a road agent. Was that hurting the project about which he had waxed so enthusiastic?

She had never seen her father that she could remember. He

had come from fully as good a Boston family as her mother, but he had never seemed to fit in the East. At least that was what her mother had said. Her other relatives had been less kind.

Betsy's mother had not been dead half a year before her father had begun to communicate with Betsy. Relatives said that he was interested in the fortune her mother had left—as her mother's purse had been trap-tight as long as she had lived. But Betsy had liked to think otherwise.

Her father had written many times that he was now an agent for the Great Western, the first railroad into Montana, but that he needed money to buy up the right-of-way in advance of construction. Puma Pass, he had said, had been selected as the only possible crossing of the Continental Divide and if he could buy this land for the railroad he would be rewarded.

It had seemed very good to Betsy. She had liked the feeling of importance his letter had given her. She had sent money and then more money and finally, as a surprise, she had come west, against all advice, to help her father in every way she could. He did not know she was coming, but in a matter of hours . . .

The brake shrieked; the coach lurched to an abrupt stop and almost threw Betsy headlong against her largest trunk, which had been too big to go outside.

She sat hastily back and righted her bonnet, while the dust caught up with the stage which had made it and curled smokily past the windows.

A voice so clear and so brutally cold that it made her tremble knifed the evening chill.

"Throw down your rifle, Bat!"

The dust thinned and Betsy, leaning sideways, looked ahead. A man on foot was standing across a newly felled tree which blocked the road. He was a terrifying sight to Betsy as he stood there balancing a huge revolver in each hand. His face was completely covered with a red bandanna into which two crude eyeholes had been cut. He was dressed in a white buckskin shirt, flaring chaps and high-heeled boots. He looked very tall, very grim.

Betsy wished fervently for Boston and its solid policemen. Up on the box were ten thousand dollars in silver and bills—her money destined for her father. And it would all be gone in an instant.

She twisted at her hat ribbon. Two bright tears welled up in her large blue eyes—tears of terror. This must be Sunset Maloney. He hated her father. What would he do when he found that she was also a Trotwood? Shoot her, most likely.

The tall man was stepping down from the tree. Bat's Winchester rattled into the dust as he dropped it.

"Now, Sunset," whined Bat. "Don't go gittin' nervous. I can't reach no higher." And in a hoarse whisper, "Git your hands up, Tom, you fool. T'hell with them horses."

"What are you carrying?" said the clear, chill voice.

"Got it right here," cried Bat, anxious to please. The express box hit the road leadenly.

"Who's inside?"

Bat would not answer that. Betsy swiftly withdrew her head from the window. He had not seen her in the dusk. She knew he would kill her just as soon as he discovered who she was. She mourned for faraway Boston. Why had she ever taken this foolish trip?

She moved swiftly across the seat, hitting her knees against her big wicker and leather trunk. In it were skirts and hats, carefully packed.

With brilliant inspiration, knowing that her fate depended upon her action, Betsy threw the trunk lid up, cast out the cardboard hat boxes and rolled hastily into the yielding mass of her piled skirts. There was just room enough with the hats out. She dropped the lid just as she heard his footsteps grating in the road beside the stage.

She heard something else. The patent locks clicked shut as the lid fell. But she had no fear. Bat would let her out as soon as the danger was past.

Sunset threw open the door, right gun ready to chop down if anyone had been waiting inside. He stood there for an instant, inspecting the place.

"Empty, huh?" said Sunset.

Bat leaned far over and looked down with jaw sagging. "Huh?" He blinked hard and leaned farther, almost falling from his high perch.

"Something wrong here," said Sunset. "You don't want me to look this over. What is it? Another messenger box?"

The stage creaked as he mounted the step. He looked at the shipping tag which had been affixed at the last outpost of the slowly advancing railroad.

"'Trotwood, Puma Pass,'" read Sunset. "So it *is* something else."

He gave the trunk a hard shove. It shot out the other door

and slammed to the ground, bottom side up. Sunset jumped down beside it and heaved it over.

"It's heavy enough," he said. Turning to look up at the box, he added, "I think that's downright thoughtless of you, Bat. You know I'm interested in anything goin' to Slim Trotwood."

"Sure," shook Bat. "Sure, Sunset. I . . . I guess I kinda forgot, that's all."

"Next time kinda remember to remember," threatened Sunset.

Deliberately he drew out a bowie knife and hacked down two small pines. He lashed these, one on either side, to his heavy rimfire saddle, making a specie of Indian travois.

Across this he placed the trunk, tying it in place with his lariat. Finishing, he turned to Bat and Tom. "When you get to Puma Pass, you tell that damned coyote Trotwood that I still aim to fight him as long as I got lead to sling and strength to pull a trigger. Savvy?"

"We told him last time and he damn near skinned us alive," complained Bat.

"Tell him again," said Sunset.

"You bet," said Bat quickly.

Sunset took his reins and led his mustang onto a game trail at right angles to the wagon road. With the trunk bumping along on the travois, he made his way between the pines, finally disappearing from view.

Tom, always short on words, growled, "You done it again."

"Can I help it?" blustered Bat. "He'd of shot me if I'd moved my little finger."

"You wouldn't be in with him, would you?" growled Tom.

"Me?" cried Bat. "In with a road agent? Why, you low-down lobo, I ought to . . ."

"Save it for a road agent," said Tom. "You better see if that girl ain't dead from heart failure."

Bat remembered then. He swung down and looked into the stage. He stuck his shaggy head inside and peered into all the corners. He looked under the wheels without result and then stood back scratching his head.

"She was here a minute ago," said Bat.

He made a complete circuit of the stage and again inspected the interior and again scratched his head. "All she left is a few hats. Now where the ding-dong do you suppose the critter went?"

Tom got down and looked with no more result than Bat. Together they walked down the grade, peering into clumps of bushes. They came back and searched the coach again.

"If that don't beat hell," said Bat. "She's gone to glory."

"Damned if she ain't," said Tom.

"Never did trust Boston nohow," said Bat, spitting into the dust. "We better get that tree outta the road and git the word to town."

A half-hour's work rid them of the tree and four hours of torturous mountain roads brought them into Puma Pass' one unpainted street.

Yellow squares from the windows fell into the restless thoroughfare. Doors swung outward when the word swept along the row of false-front buildings. Cowboy boots rapped lightly and miner's boots thumped solidly as a crowd gathered to watch the stage come in.

Tom braked to a halt before the California Saloon. Bat stood up in the glow of his box lanterns and half dismounted, shouting to the crowd:

"We lost a dame out and we been robbed! Where's Slim Trotwood, the yaller pup?"

The crowd was astounded at the first part of the news. They were silent until Bat hit dust and then they swarmed in upon him with a roar of questions.

"I tell you that's all I know," protested Bat. "We lost her out slick as a whistle. Where's Slim Trotwood?"

A thin, dark-haired man in a black frock coat was hastily let through the press. He came to a halt in the ring of light spread by the stage lanterns.

Slim Trotwood was dressed in the height of fashion. His black knee boots had a white ring around each top. His hat was a fifty-dollar John B. and his shirt was made of the finest of linen. He had a thin white face and he wore upon it a twisted smile which showed his great superiority. He spoke with a cultured Boston drawl.

"Who wanted me?"

"I did," said Bat. "We brung your daughter as far as the foothills and then all of a sudden she disappeared."

"My daughter?" said Trotwood, almost showing his surprise. "You must be mistaken, Connor. My daughter is in Boston."

"She ought to a stayed in Boston," said Bat. "You didn't have no business lettin' a cute little trick like her come all the way out to Montana."

"Be quick, man," Trotwood snapped. "Where did you lose her?"

"Now ain't that intelligent," scoffed Bat. "If I knowed where I lost her I wouldn't a lost her."

Trotwood was annoyed. "I'll have my men make a search immediately if you'll tell me the approximate location."

"Up by Sioux Canyon," said Bat. "You'll find the tree alongside the road. Yeah. I forget to tell you. We was held up."

"You mean we didn't get our money again?" said a hard voice out in the crowd.

A thick-shouldered hunched man of great height, who had the appearance of never being able to straighten up because he'd hit his head against the sky, shuffled to Trotwood's side. His red-rimmed eyes were angry.

Trotwood faced him with contempt. "You'll get your pay soon enough. The Great Western would hardly fail to pay its bills."

"I been stalled long enough," said the tall man.

"Simpson," said Trotwood, severely, "I'll have no more nonsense, if you please. You have my word. . . ."

"Your word," mocked Simpson.

Trotwood's action did not seem to be enough to warrant Simpson's hasty change in tone. Trotwood merely thrust his hand slowly into his frock coat in a Napoleonic gesture.

"Get your horses and the rest of the men," said Trotwood carefully, as though controlling himself only with great effort. "Sunset Maloney is responsible for this. This time, we are going to make him answer."

Simpson backed off, turned and shuffled toward a livery stable down the street, collecting a small knot of men as he went.

Trotwood turned to Bat. "You seem to have great difficulty in defending your charge, Connor."

"I'm brave enough," said Bat. "If that Sunset hadn't got the drop on me, I'd a blowed him fuller a holes than a Swiss cheese. Next time I meet him, he'll have a fight on his hands!"

Somebody in the crowd cried, "Wildcat Connor."

Bat turned to face the unseen attacker. "Yeah? You wouldn't a done any different."

"Wildcat Connor!"

"Yeah?" bellowed Bat. "Look here, from Texas to Oregon, I'm knowed as a lead slinger and I ain't goin' to let no sucklin' pig laugh at me without . . ."

Simpson was coming up the street with the men and Bat forgot what he was saying for the moment as he watched them.

Trotwood mounted his well-groomed horse, putting his polished toes daintily into the stirrups of his postage-stamp English saddle.

Simpson and his five hard-faced companions closed up around Trotwood, who glanced at them to see that they were all there and well armed.

"We shall proceed to Sioux Canyon," Trotwood told them, "and attempt to track him from there. I trust that we have ropes enough to do our work tomorrow."

He raised his arm and dug spur. The cavalcade rolled up the street, lights from windows flashing on bits and guns as they raced by.

The sound of hoofs faded slowly and Bat turned to tromp up the steps of the Palace Saloon, ignoring questions from the curious. He went into the smoky interior and walked down the bar, still refusing to further discuss the holdup. Men drifted away from him and he finally stood alone, pouring a drink of red liquor into a smudged glass.

When he had downed it he saw that a stranger stood beside him. The man wore range clothes much out of place upon his round, awkward body. He was unused to such clothes. His face was burned red by wind and looked soft.

"Set him up another, barkeep," said the stranger.

"Don't care if I do," said Bat.

The bartender set up several more and finally Bat found himself at a quiet table in the corner facing the stranger, who said his name was Smith.

"Who is this Sunset Maloney?" said Smith.

"Good kid," said Bat tipsily. "None better. Sure death when he's mad but easygoin' most always. Red hair makes him that way."

"Other shipments come through untouched," said Smith. "What's Sunset Maloney got against Trotwood?"

"What's everybody got against Trotwood, you mean," snapped Bat, grabbing the neck of the bottle and slopping his drink as he poured it, so great was his sudden heat.

"Well, what?"

"It's that Great Western Railroad," said Bat, tongue well greased by now. "They got to have this pass. They can't get across the Rockies at this point unless they get this pass. Puma Pass means plenty. But it's all owned. Mining claims, small ranches, truck farms to feed the miners that keep crossing back and forth here. This is the best way through the whole

dadblamed Continental Divide and the Great Western's got
to have it."

"What's that make Trotwood?"

"A polecat," said Bat. "He come in here and sized it up
and then shows his papers as agent of the Great Western.
Everybody wants the railroad but there ain't nobody wants
to sell any land, that being valuable right here. So Trotwood
hires a Texas gun-toter named Simpson and some of his
friends. Five settlers had disappeared. There ain't nobody else
willin' to argue it with Trotwood. So he's buyin' all land at
fifty percent of its value. Sell or get killed, that's the situation.
And everybody's afraid to touch him."

"Can't you organize?"

"Like them vigilantes they got over at Virginia City? We
tried it and the ringleader disappeared and now everybody's
scared to name hisself a leader."

"Where's Sunset Maloney fit into this?" said the persistent
stranger, who said his name was Smith.

"Sunset?" said Bat, settling himself and pouring another
drink. "Like I tell you, he's redheaded and easygoin' most of
the time, but he gets mad suddenlike and nothin' can stop
him when he's mad.

"He come in here right after the government reopened
the Bozeman trail. He's up from Wyoming, just a kid, fresh
as paint but broke. So old Ten-Sleep Thompson takes him
under his wing and they get along on small strikes. Pretty
soon they got enough together for a spread and for the past
ten years, they run it. It's right in the middle of this valley

below here. The longhorns was doin' well and everything was goin' fine and Sunset grows up to his present manhood of twenty-three, all grin or all fight, either way.

"And then Sunset goes to trail a herd up from Wyomin' and when he gets back, Trotwood has moved into Puma Pass. That's bad, but what Sunset finds is worse. Ten-Sleep Thompson has signed over the spread to Trotwood for cash nobody ain't seen yet, though Trotwood says it's comin'. Ten-Sleep is dead and buried when the kid arrives home.

"So he hits the trail and starts layin' for Trotwood. He stops all stages to take off any Trotwood money. He pops up unexpected when Trotwood gets too persuasive with some miner. An' if it wasn't for Sunset, this whole place would have been sold out to Trotwood a long time ago. So far, Sunset has got all the gold Trotwood tried to import, and as long as he keeps out of Trotwood's . . . Say, gabbin' around like this plumb made me fergit something mighty important. See you later, stranger."

Bat wobbled to the door and went out into the street. He made his way to his cabin but he did not enter. He went around back and began to saddle his mustang.

"Damn it to hell," muttered Bat, wrestling with the saddle and seeing three horses when he knew he only owned one, "I was goin' to take just one drink to make it look less suspicious and I get to gabbin' like an old hen at a tea party and plumb fergit Sunset. If he swings, I'll never draw another easy breath!"

The saddle slid off on the other side and Bat lurched under

the mount's neck to get it. He put it up again and it slid off on the nigh side.

Swearing at the three shimmering mustangs, Bat tried to concentrate on what he was doing.

Outlaw's Captive

FROM the moment Betsy Trotwood had lost her consciousness in the falling trunk until she awoke in the dimness of an old trapper's cabin was a complete blank.

She lay looking disinterestedly at the pattern of shadows the rafters made, trying to clear her wits and think. The last thing she had seen had been a tall man in stained leather standing on a fallen tree with a gun in each hand. Somehow that did not connect up with this.

Gradually she became aware of someone seated beside her. Slowly she turned her head to behold a man silhouetted against the flickering light given out by a piece of rag stuck into a cup of bear grease on the table across the rough room.

Even then she did not know what it was all about. Her head ached dully and the man meant nothing to her, for the moment, less than the rafter shadows.

"Gee, ma'am," said Sunset with a gusty sigh of relief, "you shore had me worried for a while. How do you feel?"

This soft drawl was not the clear and deadly voice of the road agent. She studied the silhouette curiously.

Sunset got up. "Let me get you a cup of tea," he said eagerly. "You'll be ready to fight a buzz saw before you know it."

He crossed the room to the fireplace and her eyes followed

him. He stood for an instant against the light of brightly glowing coals and abruptly she knew him.

She recoiled, pressing herself against the logs at the back of the bunk, gripping the edge of a blanket with her small hand.

Sunset, all unknowing, came back with the tin cup full of steaming tea. "Here, ma'am. Drink this."

He saw how she stared at him then. The terror in those wide blue eyes came as a shock to him. He set the cup on a three-legged stool and looked at her. "What's the matter?"

She found her voice, fought the tremble out of it. Her mother's people had given her a legacy of spirit and poise. "Thief!"

"Thief?" said Sunset. "Oh, now, see here, ma'am, don't go judging things so fast. I'm no more thief than you are, beggin' your pardon."

"I'll thank you to take me to my father instantly," said Betsy.

Sunset looked at her in hurt amazement. Her tone cut into him cruelly. But he was conscious of a lingering amusement too. She was so small and delicate that he could have lifted her with one hand but she was showing more fight than a shoulder-shot grizzly.

"See here, ma'am. I'm sorry about this. But I was just as surprised as you were. I feel pretty bad kicking you out of the stage that way, but how was I to know? And I tell you, ma'am, when I opened that trunk of yours and saw you in it, all white, I was plenty scared. I thought you were dead. You're safe, honest you are. I wouldn't hurt you. If I could I'd do anything in the world for you. You can believe that, ma'am."

She was inching further away from him than ever, cold

contempt in her gesture and expression. He could feel the intensity of her growing rage.

Clumsily he sought to quiet her. "Whatever made you get into Trotwood's trunk? That was plumb careless of you, ma'am. Somebody ought to have told you that anybody that runs up against anything belongin' to that skunk runs into sure trouble."

"Are you referring to my father?" she said frostily.

"Your father?" said Sunset. "No, ma'am. I'm talkin' about Double-Deck Trotwood, or Slim Trotwood, or any other name he goes by." In sudden wonder, seeing the way the words affected her, he said, "Say, you ain't tied up with that ornery, two-bit tinhorn, are you?"

"Sir, I'll have you know that Jonathan Trotwood is my father."

"Your *father?*" gaped Sunset. "Oh, now, see here, ma'am, that isn't anything to joke about."

"It is certainly no joke."

"You're dead right. Not if it's a fact." Sunset sat down weakly on the edge of the bunk. "Tell me straight now, ma'am. Is that weasel-faced back-stabber your dad, honest-to-God?"

"You must realize that your language is most offensive," said Betsy.

"No more offensive than your news," said Sunset wearily. He got up and tried to give her the tea again but she would have none of it. He crossed the room and threw some wood on the fire and then sat on his heels before the blaze, pulling a frying pan disconsolately toward him. She heard him mutter, "If that don't beat hell . . ."

23

In sudden wonder, seeing the way the words affected her,
he said, "Say, you ain't tied up with that ornery,
two-bit tinhorn, are you?"

Now that his presence was more remote, she sank back on the pillow he had made from a buffalo robe and looked steadily at him from the protecting darkness of the bunk.

She was very afraid, as she had every right to be. Everything about this country had filled her with uneasy awe and she had begun to understand how little she knew about the world.

The dizziness passed slowly from her and she began to consider her problem. She thought of escape but knew instantly that she was somewhere far from any habitations or towns. The way must be far and the trails alive with danger.

She wondered how much harm she could expect from this tall bandit and fell to studying his profile against the now-leaping flames.

He was young, probably in his early twenties. His face was lean and hard but there was a reckless strength to it which might have been fascinating to her in other circumstances, so different was it from the weak, white visages of the men she had danced with so lately.

His costume was strange to her. She had never seen a man dressed wholly in soft white leather before. His spurs were bright and she decided they were silver. Two pendants hung from each and clinked together, making music as he moved at his work.

Bat had called him "Sunset" and she decided that it must be because of his auburn hair.

There was a certain grace to his movements, a freedom of carriage which was suggestive of the wide free world in which he dwelt. He smelled of clean woodsmoke and pines

25

and sage, and the effect of all this combined lulled her fears which became more subdued as her interest grew.

At last her glance strayed about the cabin. Wild animal skins were nailed on the walls. Two rifles hung from pegs over the door. Buffalo robes covered the floor. A saddle and a small bundle of clothing seemed to be Sunset's only possessions outside of his guns and frying pan.

She glimpsed the messenger box under the table and suddenly she was angry again.

She looked further and beheld two other boxes, identical to the first. Three checks she had sent to a certain bank at her father's direction. These three boxes must contain seventy-five thousand dollars—half of her mother's fortune.

When Sunset finished his cooking he approached her bunk once more. The smell of the savory steak was almost too much for her to bear.

Sunset shrugged and set the plate down on the stool beside her. He filled the cup with fresh tea and then, without a glance at her, buckled on his guns and went outside.

After he had closed the door she stared at it for a long time. She had led a very closely guarded life up to now. Her emotions had been limited to joy and sorrow. But now she was amazed at the depths of anger and disappointment and fear which she found in herself.

She tried to keep the upper hand of control. But a traitor within her disclosed the fact that his disregard of her had added as much to her rage as the messenger boxes.

She lay back and became quiet. The steak beside her sent its appealing aroma over the edge of the bunk. She was hungry but she refused to eat. And then in sudden panic she was afraid the steak would get cold and sat up instantly.

In vain she looked for a fork or spoon. Only a harsh-looking bowie knife was there. She picked it up gingerly and turned it over, wondering what to do with it.

Baffled, she looked longingly at the steak. Not even as a child had she eaten with her fingers. Her well-served table had always been graced with a multitude of bright spoons and forks.

Again she remembered that the steak would get cold. Almost in tears she cautiously extended a small white hand to touch the warm, moist meat. She sat up and propped the pillow back of her.

She ate.

And when she had finished she looked helplessly about her for a napkin and, finding none, was forced to use her outraged Bostonian tongue to clean her fingertips.

She had no more than finished when she heard a far-off shot. She sat up in wide-eyed terror, wanting to go to the window but afraid to move.

Tensely she waited. The fire died down. The rag in the cup spluttered out. A beam of moonlight fell bluely to the rough floor.

Would he never come back?

She moved off the bunk hesitantly at last and crept to the window to look out. The hillside above the cabin was dotted with shaggy pines, silver green by moonlight. A stream tinkled nearby and a slow wind sighed mysteriously through the trees at hand.

Far off, thin in distance, a coyote yip-yapped at the moon and ended with a high, gradually sinking howl more awful than death itself. Another coyote answered and then the two sent their mournful voices together across the shivery night. A wolf's bass threat moaned down the scale and the coyotes howled no more.

The pines soughed softly in a cold rush of wind. The brook made its light sound against the somber breeze.

The hillside was filled with mysteriously moving shadows. Two limbs creaked dolefully together, chilling Betsy until she could not move away from the spot where she stood.

Would he *never* come back?

She heard a thump at the back of the cabin. Slow footfalls sounded. Metal clinked and the door flew open.

She whirled, pressing herself back against the logs, trembling.

It was Sunset. He looked at her strangely for a moment and then carelessly walked to the fire and began to load a pipe. He hooked a glowing coal toward him and turned part way toward her.

"Mind if I smoke?"

"No," she whispered.

He puffed thoughtfully for a moment and then began to lay limbs on the coals and fan them into a blaze. The light was warm and the strength of the man kneeling there was reassuring. Gradually the cold went away from her heart and she moved slowly sideways to sit down on the edge of the bunk.

"Got a deer at a pool below here," said Sunset carelessly.

"Hung him up on a peg behind the cabin. He ought to make good eating."

For the first time in her life it occurred to her that the meat she ate had once been alive. It came as a shock.

Unreasonably then, she was once more angry with him. "How long do you expect to keep me here?"

"Until I can send you to Puma Pass, I reckon," said Sunset, watching the fire. "Of course it's taking a chance to let you go and I hadn't ought to do it. They'll spot this place when you tell them and it's been a safe retreat until now."

"I'm sure," she said bitterly, "that I am a great deal of trouble to you."

"You sure are," said Sunset.

She glared at his fire-outlined profile.

"What about my reputation?" she said. "Have you thought of that?"

"What's the matter with it?" said Sunset.

With cool contempt she said, "Do you expect me to sleep in the same room with you?"

"Oh," said Sunset in a way which told her he was hurt.

He got up deliberately and knocked the ashes from his pipe. He went to the door and jerked a buffalo robe from the wall.

Suddenly she remembered the howling coyotes, the wolf, the soughing pines and the awful loneliness of the moonlight. "No! Don't leave me!"

"Make up your mind," said Sunset. "Do I stay or do I go?"

Meekly, but amazed at her meekness, she whispered, "You'd better stay. I'm . . . I'm afraid."

Compassion was deep in his light blue eyes. He almost moved toward her. Instead he tossed the robe on the floor and sat down upon it, facing the fire.

She climbed into the bunk and turned her face to the wall, crying silently.

CHAPTER THREE

Gun-Smoke Baptism

A T four the following afternoon, when shadows grew long and blue in the pine-scented canyon, a stone rolled sharply down the slope to land in the brook with a small splash.

Sunset had been sitting against the wall, legs crossed Indian fashion, cleaning his already burnished Colts. He sat forward, looking up and ahead, eyes alight with the awareness of danger. Mechanically his hands swung the cylinders back into place.

Betsy had not heard the stone but she could not mistake Sunset's tenseness. She sat very still on the bunk, watching, holding her breath.

With two quick strides Sunset carefully stepped to the window and peered out. Apparently the canyon was deserted. And then a blue jay began to scold high in a sighing pine. A squirrel took it up in another quarter. A magpie's black-and-white body swooped up the creek as it shrilled indignation.

"They've come for you," said Sunset. "Get down."

Betsy's words came spontaneously and at the moment she did not realize their meaning. "They'll kill you!"

"They can only attack from the front if they want to keep their cover. Lie down on the floor. A bullet might plow through that chinking."

31

The word bullet was hard reality. With an awed glance at Sunset who was still erect by the window, Betsy crouched on the floor.

Sunset took a rifle down and checked its load. He pulled the other to him and worked the lever once. She saw the bright yellow glint of the cartridge as it slid out of the magazine into the chamber. She did not miss the hardness which had come into his face or the way he stood forward on the balls of his feet, listening intently.

Then, so swiftly she could not follow the motion, he threw the rifle to his shoulder, aimed through the window and fired. The thunder of the .44 deafened her. The acrid white fumes of black powder were shredded by the wind as they blew back into the room.

Another rock rolled on the hill. Or was it a rock? It started slowly, gathered speed and sound. Metal clinked and slithered over granite and then there was a thump and splash in the creek.

Sunset casually levered the Winchester and the black-barreled empty tinkled as it hit the floor to roll smokily across the rough boards within an inch of her hand. She drew her fingers back swiftly as though they had touched the hot metal.

Looking up again at Sunset, her small face was drawn with the pain of knowledge.

He had killed a man with that bullet.

Suddenly all thought was lost in the blasting eruption of hammering guns outside. Lead smacked into the cabin walls, ricocheted from the open window to scream through the room with the sound of a broken banjo string.

She hugged the floor. The louder concussions came from Sunset's .44 Winchester. She was choked with the biting smoke, dizzy with the intensity of the noise. A bullet whacked into the bunk just above her head and a splinter of wood twitched at her yellow hair. She felt very small, very vulnerable as she pressed her face against the floor.

The sudden, savage brutality of this battle had left her dazed. There had been no prelude. Men were striving to kill men in the quickest possible time. There would be no quarter here.

Sunset stabbed slugs into the pall of smoke which drifted above the ridge of the canyon. As he changed rifles he caught a glimpse of the girl and for an instant his expression softened.

"Poor kid," he muttered.

And then, as he fired, he found himself assailed by the strange impossibility of his position. Trotwood was up there on the ridge trying to kill him. He was shooting at Trotwood, this girl's father, hoping that any slug might find a home in Double-Deck Trotwood's heart.

He thought he heard a hail and stopped firing. In an instant all was silent in the canyon, and Sunset, looking across the creek, out of which two upturned boots protruded, felt the insecurity of his position. He could not kill Trotwood as long as she thought her father was worthy.

"Maloney!" came Trotwood's voice, thin in the distance. "Send her out or we'll come down and get her ourselves!"

Sunset turned. "That's your father talking, ma'am."

She lifted her blanched countenance to his. "What would they do if I went?"

"Keep hammering at me. You'd better go."

As he watched her throw her jacket about her shoulders, he felt empty and heartsick. He had no claim upon her and she was going to leave him without speaking again.

What would Trotwood do to her?

His voice sounded flat and dry. "Are you responsible for sending this money into Puma Pass?"

She was almost to the door. She stopped. "Yes."

"Then he's bleeding you for what you've got. Don't let him have any more. Wait. You don't know what might happen to you, ma'am. He's a skunk. You don't know him. You've never . . ."

"Please."

Sunset shrugged. He should not let her go. He ought to hold her as a hostage, use her to trap Trotwood.

But he couldn't.

She had the door half open as she turned again. She saw he was not watching her. He was staring up at the ridge and his knuckles were white as he gripped the hot Winchester.

Her voice was small, "Goodbye."

He did not face her again or answer her. He heard the door close, saw her walk across the clearing, saw her recoil from the boots which stuck up out of the creek, watched her as she balanced herself over the log bridge. She vanished into the pines. Twice after that he glimpsed her bright, full skirt as she ascended the windy slope. Then she disappeared over the rim.

A moment later, guns started up on the ridge.

Sunset sighted a dark hat and hoped as he pulled the trigger.

A man in a red shirt sprang backwards into view and began to roll downward, starting a small avalanche. It was not Trotwood.

He had watched for a moment, exposed to view. A jagged stab of lightning ripped through his shoulder. His hand let go the Winchester stock and he could not lift his arm. He looked down at the bright gush of blood which stained the buckskin of his shirt. Again he tried to lift his arm and could not.

Up above they must have realized something of this.

Sunset sat down on her wicker trunk. He picked up a petticoat with his good left hand. He started to tear it and then stopped. He laid it carefully back and walked painfully to the small package of his own clothes. He took out a scarlet headsilk and began to wind it around his shoulder, tightly, so that the artery would be stopped.

He looked up through the window. Two men were coming carefully down the slope, guns ready, walking crouched, eyes beady under the flat brims of their wide hats.

Betsy watched them go down. Trotwood had not given orders. He had merely nodded and Simpson and another man had started. And then Trotwood had watched. Something in the blackness of his eyes had chilled her.

He had said no word of greeting. He had not asked her if she was all right. He had merely nodded and the two men had started down.

"They'll kill him," she whispered, almost to herself.

"Yes," said Trotwood.

"Won't . . . won't he have a trial?"

Trotwood faced her, amused. "A trial? Oh, well, I suppose I was as green as you when I first came out. There's neither

35

judge nor policeman within half a thousand miles. I say, you aren't sympathizing with him, are you? After all, my dear, he's a bandit, a murderer, and you're lucky to get away from him so easily. He has almost put a stop to my operations here, using some silly pretext or other. He has seventy-five thousand dollars of your money down there. We must get it back, you know."

"Do you *have* to kill him?" she said.

Trotwood's scrutiny of her was more puzzled than before. But he was too wise to press her for her reasons. It worried him, a little, the way she looked down at the cabin from between the cleft in the rocks. She was an uncommonly beautiful young woman, blond as her mother and quite as charming. Strange to see her against this setting of pines and gun smoke. Why had the little fool come?

Simpson and the other had reached the creek and Trotwood was eagerly giving them all his attention. He was glad to let them do this work for him. It was not a matter of bravery with Trotwood, but of authority. He had made a reputation already in other parts of the West as an excellent shot and a fast draw from a shoulder holster.

No shots came from the cabin and Betsy felt the dread within her increase until it lay like lead upon her heart. She could not understand why she felt this way; she did not try to understand.

Simpson started over the bridge.

Suddenly a bullet geysered in the stream under his feet. He hurriedly scuttled back into the shelter of the pines. His companion looked wonderingly at the cabin.

"It didn't come from there," said Simpson.

"It's a trap!"

Simpson tried to stifle the growing desire to run. He did not know where the next one would strike. They might even have their backs to this unseen marksman.

Another shot showered Simpson with bark.

He ducked and glanced up to see powder smoke hanging on the opposite canyon rim.

An instant later three rapid shots blasted straight from rim to rim. Two more ripped into the depths of the canyon.

The targets ducked hastily. He raised himself now to peer across the canyon. He could not see the sniper nor could he understand why the sniper was there. A bullet snapped viciously overhead and Trotwood's hat went sailing up and back. He ducked anew.

A loud, rough voice from nowhere bellowed, "C'mon, Sunset! I'll keep the lobos down!"

Bat laid down another barrage from the vantage point of the rim. He kept his Winchester hot as he churned the earth and wood around Simpson and his companion, the stone and dust about Trotwood and the other man above.

Nobody saw Sunset leave the cabin.

When the firing stopped, Sunset's horse was gone and only a scattered pile of empties marked the spot where Bat had lain.

Disgusted and out of temper, Trotwood loaded the three messenger boxes, the unwanted girl and his two dead men, and started back to Puma Pass.

37

CHAPTER FOUR

Murder Threat

FOR two months, Betsy Trotwood heard nothing of Sunset Maloney and the chill of the fall which came early to these high mountains seeped into her heart.

At first she had argued unceasingly with herself against the unreasoning love she knew she bore for the tall, flame-haired frontiersman. She told herself that it was the drama she had experienced with him. She added that it was the strangeness of his type which had attracted her. But no amount of hereditary calm could talk down the fact that she did love him, bandit and killer though he might be.

The night she had found herself alone in the cabin had become symbolical of what he meant to her. In Puma Pass she was out of place and felt it keenly. She seemed to dwell at some distance from the town and though broad hats were always tipped and men made way for her with gallantry wherever she went, she could feel the bars between herself and these hard-living Westerners. They treated her with much restraint for two reasons. She was a "good woman," the first to come to Puma Pass, and she was the daughter of Slim Trotwood, otherwise Double-Deck, otherwise Boston Slim, whose reign in the mountains had become intolerable.

With cash in his pockets, with Simpson and a dozen hard-lipped gunmen at his back, Trotwood was buying up the pass right-of-way, foot by foot, for miles on either side of the range. Deed after deed found its way into his pocket. Now and then men were missing, but no one dared ask how or why. Great Western, said Trotwood smoothly, had to have the right-of-way and mere settlers could not stand in its steel path. He paid fifty percent of the recognized value and men accepted it, knowing the fate of others.

Trotwood's black frock coat, flowing tie and white-topped boots were always an occasion for whispers and sullen stares in Puma Pass. But Trotwood told them bluntly that with all of unsettled Montana for range, men should not feel badly about giving up their few acres in the Continental Divide. The Oregon Trail trade, which was prospering, meant nothing to him but much to Puma Pass.

And though Betsy might sense some of this, she had no reason to feel suspicious of her father. To her he was cool and polite as a gentleman from Boston might be expected to be.

Even the promise of riches he had given her when she had first come had been delivered with well-bred restraint. Boston Slim Trotwood could be most convincing, especially so to this small young lady who had arrived so unexpectedly and whose arrival had been so financially welcome.

While there was still another seventy-five thousand dollars in her mother's estate, Betsy did not need to worry about her treatment at Trotwood's hands. It would be excellent.

At the end of the first month, he had requested additional capital. And, mistaking the restraint of the town toward him for respect, seeing how well he was doing, she could not refuse.

Two weeks later he had required more and he had received

it via stage and the bank at Virginia City, to which the funds were relayed from the East.

She had felt no alarm at the dwindling numbers in her account book. They were numbers only and she knew nothing of finance. She experienced a certain excitement at being so important to Trotwood's undertaking.

And then, a week before, she had written the last check she was able to write, not in the least alarmed at the fact that she was now penniless, two thousand miles from home, in a strange land which seemed to want to keep her a stranger. Trotwood had been very certain of swift returns. He would double her money in a month.

She sat, at evening, at the window of the crudely furnished cabin which fronted the town's only street. The long mountain dusk had faded into the lamplighted night. A train of emigrants had left the dust stirring lazily in the road as they went to their camping ground higher in the pass. Scouts in buckskin, cowboys in high-heeled boots, cavalrymen in blue, mud-spattered miners all mingled in the parade which passed her door. But Sunset was not there.

She turned as Trotwood entered the dim room and watched him light the table lamp. Her skirt of pale blue silk rustled as she stood.

"The stage came in a moment ago," Trotwood informed her.

"Was . . . was it held up?" she said, hiding the eagerness in her voice.

"No. Maloney must have died or left the country."

The light was too dim for him to see the sadness of her small face.

41

"We have all of it now," he continued. "Tonight I shall close the last deal."

"And then we'll leave this place?"

He shrugged and went to his desk. She wondered a little at his curtness as it was unusual for him. She sat down, watching him write lengthily and listening to the scratch of his pen.

Again she turned to the street, watching for a buckskin shirt and a wide hat in this passing multitude. It seemed as though all the West was going past her door, but the only portion of it she desired was not there.

So deep was her concentration that she did not hear Trotwood rise from his chair and leave. She was startled to see him crossing the dusty street, shouldering through the crowd, as she thought he was still behind her. By the light which streamed in square pillars from a saloon door, she saw him stop Simpson and give him a letter. The instructions were long and Trotwood seemed very careful about them. He went on into the saloon and Simpson turned to his horse at a hitch rack and forked leather.

She watched Simpson depart. Two more of Trotwood's men swung up the saloon steps and went in. They came out a little later, crossed the street and walked toward another saloon.

She heard their voices through her open window.

"About time we was paid off."

"Yeah, I'm dead for a spree. Where next, Peewee?"

"Oregon, I guess. Plenty gunwork over the mountains."

They went out of her sight and she sat puzzling over what they had said. Trotwood was through here but she felt oddly about this payoff. It was strange to have another spend her money without consulting her. Still, as she always told herself, he was her father and he needed her help.

The night air was growing colder and she moved to the fireplace and laid sticks on the coals. Doing that gave her pain, somehow, and yet there was pleasure in that pain. Sunset had done that.

She sat back, watching the blaze fan to life, thinking far thoughts. What was it she had seen in that frontiersman? She had been with him for such a short time. And yet it seemed, in retrospect, that she had lived with him for months, even years.

Dwelling upon his image, her head sank further back against the chair. She dozed fitfully, waking at long intervals to put more wood upon the fire. And then a change in the tone of the street roused her.

Puma Pass, always noisy after dark, began to double its volume. Something was happening out there.

She got up and hurried to the window, throwing back the shutter to look out. Men were standing in small groups talking or hurrying down the street or up the street to get into other groups, talk and then hurry onward.

Presently two horsemen came riding through the yellow patches of light from the east. No. One horseman. The other mount had something dark dangling from either side of the saddle.

She stepped back with an involuntary gasp as the mustangs walked slowly past. Simpson's body was lashed over his saddle.

The horseman, one of Trotwood's riders, pulled up before the Palace Saloon. In an instant the collected crowd opened on either side of the doors and Trotwood's tall black silhouette stood on the porch against the light.

The crowd was still.

"It's Simpson," said the rider.

Trotwood took one step down and stopped. "Who killed him?"

"He was headin' out of town," said the rider, "and I met up with him and offered to go along. We went about half a mile when a feller rode out in front of us and stopped. Simpson told him to get out of the way but he wouldn't budge. We recognized him both at the same time and Simpson drawed. But he wasn't fast enough. Sunset Maloney drilled him twice before he hit ground."

"What were you doing?" said Trotwood acidly.

"What *could* I do?" protested the rider.

"Did Maloney examine the body?"

"Sure. He took a letter out of Simpson's pocket."

"And you let him get away with it?"

"What could *I* do?"

Trotwood stepped down beside the horse and gruesome burden. He ran his hands into Simpson's pockets and brought them forth empty. He walked back up the steps and turned at the top.

"Somebody get a shovel and bury him."

He went on inside the saloon.

Betsy closed the shutters and turned to the fire which seemed cold and gray. She sat down and stared long at the dying embers, trying not to think.

The street noises faded as the excitement decreased and were again normal. She did not hear them. She heard nothing.

But suddenly she looked up and there was Sunset standing beside her chair, looking at her.

She was startled but she showed none of it. Her poise was her mother's, too great to be shaken easily.

"You came back," she said.

"I had to come back," replied Sunset.

He relaxed a little and sat on his heels before the fire, tossing sticks on the coals. She looked down on the broad expanse of his buckskin-covered back. She had thought she would challenge him for the murder of Simpson but she did not. She could think of only one thing. He cared enough to dare all this to come to her.

"I been having a hard time of it," said Sunset in a soft drawl. "You sure messed things up, ma'am. Long as I could keep money out of his hands, I had him licked. But when I found out it was your money, I couldn't take it. So I been layin' off, waiting for my chance. I hate to have to come to you saying these things. I'd rather be saying things a whole lot easier to take."

He was not looking at her. He was troubled. She wanted to reach out and touch the shoulder fringe of his shirt.

"You ain't packed up, ma'm."

"Should I be?"

"Accordin' to the stars, it's close to midnight. I had to hurry for fear you'd be gone. But you don't seem to be leavin' with him."

45

"With my father?"

"Yes. Have you . . . did you give him *all* your money?"

"Of course."

"I see. You got any idea about what you'll do if he leaves you flat in Puma Pass?"

"Why should that be necessary? If he leaves, he'll take me with him."

"Nothing can shake your faith in him?"

"He's my father."

"God shore plays some funny tricks sometimes." Sunset stirred the coals and the heated sticks blazed up, crackling, painting his strong profile with light.

"I had ideas, ma'am. I'm a presumin' cuss. I thought maybe something would happen to straighten this out. But nothin' has. He's got deeds to the right-of-way. He's bought out everybody at a shameful price and killed them that wouldn't sell. . . ."

"Please."

He pivoted to look at her face. "I had ideas. I thought maybe you would think as much of me as I have of you. But I couldn't expect that. You wouldn't touch me. You've seen me kill men. You know what I am. And no amount of arguing could ever convince you otherwise. I'm not worthy to touch the hem of your skirt. But that's not sayin' I won't take the right to help you."

In alarm she could not explain, she said, "What do you mean?"

He threw more sticks on the flames and they leaped eagerly upward to light the whole room. Sunset stood up. His spurs jingled and his cartridge belts creaked. His right-hand gun was on the level of her eyes.

She could feel the strength of him.

Sunset's voice was quiet. "I tried to tell you that he's Double-Deck Trotwood. You won't believe me. Right now, he's aimin' to walk out of Puma Pass and leave you helpless and broke. He ain't goin' to leave."

"Sunset!"

"He can take care of himself. I tell you he's Double-Deck Trotwood, fast as a strikin' rattler with his shoulder gun. You needn't worry about the odds."

She was on her feet, eyes wide as she tried to find ways to protest. But she was too much afraid of his strength, of the way he stood there.

Sunset walked to the door. "I'm sorry it had to end this way, ma'am. I wanted it otherwise. But it's my last card."

"Sunset!"

He was gone.

CHAPTER FIVE

Sunset's Return

THE man who said his name was Smith was watching
Trotwood. He was too intent to notice the precise
moment Bat Connor slid into a seat at his table. He became
aware of Bat when Connor helped himself to a drink from
Smith's bottle.

Smith expressed no surprise. "You've been gone quite a
while."

"Two awful dry months," said Bat.

"Any reason you come back just now?"

"You're full of questions," said Bat. He drank and then
wiped his whiskers with the back of his hand. "Keep yore
eyes peeled and you'll know why I'm back."

"Sunset is in town?"

"You almost got him killed once, detainin' me."

"You don't seem to be very scared about getting caught.
Everybody knows," said Smith.

"Sure they do." Bat poured himself another drink but it
was never downed.

Trotwood had been standing at the far end of the bar,
talking with a worried and sagging rancher. Money had just
changed hands and a deed had just been signed. Trotwood's
hold on Puma Pass was at last complete.

Others were lined along the mahogany in easy poses but now a ripple of tension ran down the brass-railed length. Man nudged neighbor and all faces were toward the door for one long, appalling instant.

Sunset had stepped into the big, smoky room. When he was two paces inside he stopped, hands carefully away from his guns, stiff-brimmed hat on the back of his head, flame-colored hair almost in his eyes. Then, even the fringes on his shirt stopped swinging.

Trotwood faced around and stiffened. He put both feet solidly upon the floor and was motionless.

With one concerted dive the pathway between them was cleared. A table crashed and then everybody stopped, leaving a space the width of a bowling alley between the two.

Bat carefully laid his six-gun on the table before him. Smith's eyes were critical.

A big clock above the bar ticked with agonizing monotony, loud all out of proportion.

Sunset's voice was clear and controlled. "A couple months ago, you wanted to get me pretty bad, Double-Deck. You got your chance now."

Trotwood was not afraid. His short gun had been the winner too many times, and even though this range was long for him, he knew what he could do. It showed on his face as his thin mouth relaxed into a contemptuous smile.

Abruptly Trotwood's hand stabbed inside his coat. A badly sewn button flew. Before men could realize he had moved, his short gun glittered, swinging level.

Sunset's hands flashed across his body as he snapped into a crouch. Cocked by their weight as they came free, his big Colts boomed together, their crashing thunder swallowing up the one short bark of Trotwood's gun.

Smoke swept forward toward a common meeting point and then slowly down to swirl with decreasing density. It rose upward.

Trotwood sagged against the bar, clutching at the edge. He let himself down slowly, pulling a long sheet of paper with him. His grip was tenacious, and even after he slumped to the floor, he still had the paper, redly dyed, the stain growing out toward the word *Deed*.

Nobody moved, even then, and the big clock ticked with loud, progressive regularity in the smoky silence.

Light, hurrying footsteps on the steps outside broke the spell. Betsy swung the shuttered door open and stared down the room, hand at her throat.

Sunset shoved his guns back into holsters. There was dark misery in his eyes.

He went past her and into the street. Voices babbled behind him as he strode along. Men gave him all the road there was, wishing they had nerve enough to speak to him and tell him of their gratitude.

People were surging toward the Palace Saloon. Men who had owned land and miners who had owned claims, raced eagerly to find out if it was really so, if Trotwood's power had been broken by a bullet, what chance there was of recovering what had been lost.

51

Sunset heard none of it. He reached the edge of town and mounted his waiting horse. Wearily he walked the mount down the trail and into the darkness.

Bat Connor and the man who said his name was Smith took care of Betsy. They met no resistance from her when they led her across the road to the cabin. She did not seem to be aware of them or of her own whereabouts. She sank down in a chair before the fire and the blaze was dying low.

She knew dully that the stranger and Bat Connor were talking, and though she heard it clearly she could make nothing of their words, nor did she have the energy to try.

And then they were on either side of her. Bat took a letter back from Smith and held it before her face.

"See there!" said Bat. "There's the proof! It's in his own handwriting!"

She saw it and wondered if it was the one he had written such a short time before, but nothing could excite her interest now.

"Listen to it," said Bat. He read:

President
Great Western Railroad
Dear Sir;

It gives me great pleasure to inform you, sir, that I am in possession of all lands in and adjacent to Puma Pass. Though I am not known to you, I know you will be interested. I have it on good authority that within a year you will contemplate building over the Continental Divide and I know that this is the one pass which you will find feasible. It will come as a shock to you, of course, that this land is already held. But your shortsightedness is my gain. I am leaving some hours after the bearer and will arrive close on the heels of this letter. To facilitate this transaction, you will have a hundred and fifty thousand dollars ready to place to my credit in a Chicago bank. This is of the utmost necessity as I am in something of a hurry. My price will go up in direct ratio to any delay.

Sincerely,
Jonathan Trotwood

"He was going to pull out at midnight tonight," said Smith. "I heard him tell his men as he paid them off. He was going to leave you as he had no further use for you and he was joking about it to the bartender."

Betsy looked up at the two tense faces, trying to understand what they were saying.

"I . . . I don't believe it."

Bat looked appealingly at Smith. "Tell her who you are, like you just told me."

Smith looked at Betsy for a moment, wondering about the advisability of furthering the effect of this shock.

Finally he said, very gently, "Miss Trotwood, I am a United States deputy marshal. I came here at the request of Wells Fargo to arrest Sunset Maloney. But I had to use my own judgment. I have been watching Trotwood ever since I arrived. He did nothing flagrantly lawless and in a wild country such as this, it is impossible to police all crimes, even if they were in my jurisdiction, which they are not. I have checked on Trotwood. He is known as Double-Deck or as Boston Slim. He started years ago as a card sharp, went to gambling for higher stakes, was known as a bad man with a gun. He murdered a woman at Abilene last spring and came out here to force this railroad deal and get away from the local authorities.

"When I arrived I heard about Sunset from Mr. Connor and I decided to clear up some other business and let Sunset clear up Trotwood if he could. I had no orders to do anything about it but I have to use my judgment."

"See?" crowed Bat. "Look. When Sunset laid eyes on you, out of respect for Trotwood bein' your father, he quit cold, knowin' he was stealin' your money, not Trotwood's. When he was healin' up, he used to worry about it all the time. And then he decided to nail Trotwood and save you. But the only way he could do it was by killin' Trotwood. See? If he'd thought less of you, he'd maybe have kidnapped you again or somethin'. See?"

They both stared expectantly at Betsy.

She looked very small in that big chair, very much alone.

Smith spoke again. "You are Trotwood's heir and though the deeds are in his name, they're now all yours. After what he has done to this country, the least you can do is carry on. Sunset tried and succeeded in a measure. But you hold the winning hand, miss. You better drive a bargain with the Great Western Railroad. I'll help you. A half a million for this land would be about right. And then you could take out what you put into it and hand out the money that's really coming to the original owners. They all ought to share in that profit and there's families that have other reasons to get a bigger chunk. We'll carry it out. All you have to do is sign the papers."

Wearily, she nodded, staring into the graying ashes of the fireplace.

Sunset was washing on the bank of the stream near the trapper's cabin, only partly warmed by the dying sunlight of the afternoon, listening to the brook running at his feet.

For ten days he had waited with waning hope, but now he knew that he had waited in vain. The taste of his late victory over Trotwood was a stale, even bitter thing. The price he had paid for that victory had been too great.

Ten-Sleep Thompson had been revenged, but revenge is at best an unsavory thing.

In the morning he would throw his saddle on his mount and tie his scant belongings there. Oregon was over the Divide and perhaps in Oregon he could forget.

She had never been meant for him. Who was he to aspire to such heights? He could never hope to interest her. He was rough, lacking the polish of the men to whom she had been accustomed in the East.

His reverie was interrupted by Bat's shout on the rim. Bat dismounted and led his horse down through the pines on the slope, dropping the reins and crossing the narrow bridge.

Sunset tried to cover up his bleak thoughts with a grin but the attempt was worse than his soberness.

"I knew I'd find you here," said Bat.

They shook hands and Sunset led the way into the cabin. He slid a pail of water into the ashes and began to kindle a fire about it to make Bat some welcoming tea. His tongue burned with questions but he knew that he could not bear the answers about Betsy.

Bat dropped his saddlebags to the floor, and then turned back to the door, saying, "I'll get you some wood, Sunset."

Sunset blew on the coals, adding shavings. A feeble flame flickered up. He put another stick on and followed it with a larger. The fire began to burn brightly as it picked up. Sunset added more fuel, exhausting his stock.

He heard a footstep inside the door and turned to direct Bat in the task of laying down the wood.

He opened his mouth to say a word but the word was never uttered.

Betsy was standing just inside, smiling at him.

Sunset rocked back on his heels, eyes popping with amazement. And then a big grin swept down across his face and he leaped up.

She advanced toward him, laughing, and he caught her up in his arms, smothering her in the fringe of his shirt. He put her back away from him to look at her. But try as they might they could not trust themselves to speak.

Behind them the fire caught. The gay flames crackled as they danced a bright cotillion. . . .

When Gilhooly Was
in Flower

Chapter One

JIGSAW GILHOOLY was a thousand miles deep in thought, which fact was not particularly endearing him to Mary Ann Marlow. He sat on her front porch, looked off into the purple expanses and gnawed upon a wheat straw. He looked idiotic when he sat like that, thought Mary Ann. His eyes got out of focus, and he was limp enough normally, but now...

Apparently he was a sober-faced, gangling walking stick of a puncher without any sense of humor. But Gilhooly had ideas. He had big ideas. And right now he was wondering just how to get around to fixing life so that he could ask Mary Ann to be his forevermore.

It all required considerable logic and when it came to mathematical reasoning, Jigsaw Gilhooly was aces up, though sometimes the least bit slow.

Disgustedly, Mary Ann, who taught school to the three kids in Gunpowder Gulch, picked up her copy of *Ivanhoe* and tried to read to get her mind off the way Gilhooly looked when he was jigsawing. Most of the men in the Painted Buttes country had told her she was beautiful. She believed them, a little, and therefore it grieved her that Gilhooly paid such scant attention. Most of the men in the Painted Buttes country had told her that she was a fool for seeing anything in Jigsaw Gilhooly as he had neither looks nor fortune nor reputation, and blonde little Mary Ann was beginning to believe them, a little.

Gilhooly sat and chewed his straw and focused his eyes on the back of his head, thus circumnavigating the globe with a blink.

His problem was somewhat complex. He had three hundred acres of his own and a square mile of range rented. He had forty head of cattle. He had a house which could stand both straightening and improvement. Several gentlemen had lately offered him a fancy price and he thought maybe he ought to sell and get another place before he asked Mary Ann.

And that was not all. These gentlemen were sheepmen. If sheep got a foothold on the Painted Buttes range, there wouldn't be any stopping them.

Now it was either asking Mary Ann to marry on two dollars and staying loyal to his kind or it was asking Mary Ann to marry on fifteen hundred dollars and going in debt for a place good enough for her.

So the problem shifted back and forth and so did the straw and Gilhooly kept his eyes on the back of his head via China.

"Stop it!"

Gilhooly looked at her in astonishment.

"Stop looking like a shorthorn!" said Mary Ann. "Jigs Gilhooly, sometimes I think you are a fool and at other times I am certain of it."

"Ma'am?" said the startled Gilhooly.

"Why don't you be a man?" demanded Mary Ann, blue

eyes flashing. "Why do you have to sit and moon about some crazy problem when you rode fifteen miles to see *me*?"

"That's right," said Gilhooly.

"What's right?" said Mary Ann.

"I did ride fifteen miles to see you," said Gilhooly.

She subsided, beaten. *Ivanhoe* was clutched in her small desperate hand and she felt like throwing it at him.

"Now you're mad," said Gilhooly. "I didn't mean to do anything. What's wrong?"

"Oh," said Mary Ann in a small voice. And then, sitting up like a cottontail and looking earnestly at him, "The trouble with you, Jigs Gilhooly, is that you aren't romantic!"

"Me?"

"You."

"But . . ." He stopped, baffled. "What do you mean, romantic?"

"Like Brian du Bois-Guilbert or Ivanhoe or—"

"Like who? Nobody by them names has a spread around here."

"Of course they haven't!" said Mary Ann. "Their outfits were over in England and France and places."

"Huh," said Gilhooly. "Foreigners."

"Foreigners or not, Jigs Gilhooly, if you ever expect me to pay any attention to any offer you might have to make, you'll have to mend your ways. And that's final."

"You mean be romantic?" said Gilhooly. "But . . . but gee, Mary Ann, I don't know anything about it."

An inspiration hit her. She closed the book with a thump

and handed it to him. "When you've read this, you can come and see me again—and not until!"

Gilhooly was routed. He took the book as though it had a rattler between the covers and held it away from him, looking at it. But when he looked back at Mary Ann, he could see with but half an eye that she meant what she said.

This was a new angle to the problem. He hadn't thought about her not wanting to marry him.

But the solution was offered. He would have to read this book and be romantic.

He tipped his hat. "Yes, ma'am." And backed off the porch.

He climbed his mustang, Calico, tipped his hat again to Mary Ann and neck-reined away to proceed down the wagon tracks through the sagebrush.

When he was a mile or so from the house, still in view behind him, he told Calico, "Pick your own gopher holes to fall into. I got some studyin' to do."

And so it was that Jigsaw Gilhooly began to read of the days when "Knighthood was in Flower."

"Pick your own gopher holes to fall into.
I got some studyin' to do."

Chapter Two

TWO bits' worth of midnight oil later, Jigs Gilhooly guided Calico onto the field of honor. Pennons fluttered and queens waved and armor flashed all about him. Mary Ann threw a glove toward him for an amulet and then, drawing up and lowering the shade of his visor, he glared through the slits at Brian du Bois-Guilbert who stood snorting evilly on the other side of the tilt course.

It happened, at this time, that a gentleman by the name of Fallon, who was known for determination, and his friend Billings Dwight topped the bluff above the Gilhooly ranch.

"What the devil?" said Fallon thickly, pulling in and staring.

Billings Dwight stared, too. "He must be plumb loco, Fallon. Maybe I better potshot him with this Sharps, huh?"

"Put it away," said Fallon.

Below them in a flat field, Gilhooly sat upon a much-altered Calico. A fly net decked the horse, but that was not the most astonishing thing about the ensemble. Gilhooly had a long pine pole in his hand with something which looked like a boxing glove on the far end. He had twisted his holster around so that he could couch this crude lance. On his head he had a water pail with holes in front and something which appeared to be a hearse plume bobbing above it.

Thirty yards away a longhorn bull pawed earth and blew

and was not particularly aware that he was no one but Brian du Bois-Guilbert.

Sir Gilhooly tensed in his saddle and lowered the lance. He jabbed spur to a nervous Calico and they lunged ahead, straight at the longhorn.

Calico's hoofs thundered, Sir Gilhooly yelled. The bull started a rolling charge of his own.

Two irresistible forces met in midflight. The lance hit the bull's shoulder just as the longhorn swerved.

The impact picked Sir Gilhooly out of the saddle like a pebble from a slingshot. And then, like a pole-vaulter's pole, it arced Sir Gilhooly through the air. He swooped to a loud landing thirty feet beyond the longhorn.

The bull turned; he saw his man dismounted. He started to charge, horns lowered.

But Calico was a trained cow pony and like all such, riderless or no, he would ride down a bull. He streaked in from the right, shoulder to shoulder with the racing longhorn.

The bull was not bright. He thought this was another rider. He swerved away and Calico dived in toward Sir Gilhooly who grabbed the horn and swung aboard. He reached down and scooped up the lance and bucket, then scowled at the bull.

"That's only ten times," said Gilhooly. "But, Sir Brian, we shalt meet in mortal combat yet again."

Up on the ridge Fallon and Billings Dwight were agape with wonder.

"I tell you," said Billings, "that I better pick him off before he—"

"Naw," said Fallon, scrubbing his bluish jaw. "No murder in this deal—yet."

They spurred forward and trotted down into the pasture.

Somewhat confused, Gilhooly turned to meet them. He didn't know what to do with the lance and made a useless attempt to hide the twenty-foot pine stick behind his back.

"Hello," said Fallon, cautiously.

Gilhooly nodded. He did not like sheepmen and he especially did not like Billings Dwight and Fallon. But just now he was red of face.

"Yeah?" said the late Sir Gilhooly.

"Gilhooly," said Fallon, "we come over to see if you was going to sell this place and give us that lease."

"I ain't decided," said Gilhooly.

"You mean you won't?" said Fallon.

"Well . . . I been thinking it over. It would be a damned shame to let sheep on this range. I got the only water for twenty-five miles around that's worth anything. All the cattlemen have to use my wells and if they was sheep on this place, the cows wouldn't come within a mile of the troughs if they was dyin' of thirst. Fallon, I think maybe it would be a mistake to let you have this place for any money."

Fallon stayed the black rage which began to rise within him. "You know what might happen to you, Gilhooly."

"Maybe," said Gilhooly, "but it'd take more'n a pair of buzzards to do it."

Fallon turned to his friend. "Come on, Billings. He's crazier than we thought."

As they rode away they were conscious of Gilhooly's eyes upon their backs.

"Think he's nutty?" said Billings.

"Naw," said Fallon, black eyes narrow. "It's that Mary Ann Marlow. That's my guess—and I think it's right."

"Say," said Billings, pushing his shabby hat over his brow, "you don't want no murder because we got to keep our noses clean or we won't get jack advanced."

"Yeah. No murder," said Fallon.

"And if we can get Gilhooly's wells, we can buy out the rest of this range for a song because the jack will be coming fast and we can hire a young army to keep the punchers off'n us."

"Yeah," said Fallon. "What you drivin' at?"

"Well, we got to force Gilhooly and we can't kill him. But there ain't no statute about kidnapin' around here that I ever heard of—only murder."

"Hmm," said Fallon.

"And as Gilhooly is crazy about this Mary Ann Marlow—"

"You don't have to draw pictures," snapped Fallon. "If we do that we can force Gilhooly to sell—and shut his mouth afterwards by telling him the cattlemen are out to hang him for makin' the sale. That's a good idea, don't you think so, Billings?"

Billings Dwight was enough of a diplomat to let Fallon keep the change: He only nodded.

"Now let's see. Next Sunday she'll be home from that school and nobody will be around. We walk in there— Say, we better get Stogie and Carson to come along and help. Gilhooly might walk in. He goes and sees her Sundays sometimes."

"Yeah," said the diplomat Billings, "that's a good idea, Fallon."

Chapter Three

IT was Sunday morning and the trees were singing and the birds were shining and the sun was in bloom and Sir Gilhooly trotted along on Ye Calico toward Ye Toweres of Marlowe.

As he went, he couched his lance and picked a sleeping rattler off a rock and threw the startled reptile about ninety feet away.

A horned toad also got an aerial trip and Gilhooly was pretty proud of his prowess. True, he was black and blue all over from his encounters with Brian du Bois-Guilbert and the tin pail was dented badly—and was frying hot in the desert sun—but that made no difference.

The red-bound copy of *Ivanhoe* was in his saddle-bag and Lady Mary Ann was due for a big and wondrous surprise.

If this was being romantic, it was all right with Jigsaw Gilhooly.

In the far distance he could see the house and he trotted along for three miles or so, observing it closely to make certain that Mary Ann had neither family at home nor callers. Usually the Marlows went to church over in Gunpowder Gulch, but Mary Ann did so much platform work during the week herself that she always took off Sunday as her own day of rest.

In jubilance at the final discovery that the place was

deserted, Gilhooly spurred Calico to a trot and picked up a Gila monster with his lance. When the spiny gentleman hit, he sat up and stuck out his tongue and tromped around in a circle, showing indignation.

Sir Gilhooly arrived before the clapboard Toweres of Marlowe, pointed his lance at the sizzling zenith and cried, "Hist, Ladye Mary Anne!" and then, more loudly, "How now?"

The weather-beaten old house remained quiet. Gilhooly raised his voice and repeated and then, in sudden doubt, "Hey, Mary Ann, it's just me!"

And still nothing happened.

Puzzled, Gilhooly said, "You see anything of her, Calico?"

Calico stirred and swished at the flies. Gilhooly anchored him to the wind and got down, thrusting his lance into the earth. He went into the house and stood while his eyes adjusted themselves to the dim interior.

And then his glance lighted upon a tidy out of place. That would never happen in Mrs. Marlow's house. Again, there was some dust upon the floor and . . .

He got down on his knees and picked up a torn bit of gingham. A flood of unreasoning terror took him. He jumped to his feet and stared all about him. He went swiftly to the kitchen and there he found a chair overturned. Just outside the back door he saw that the loose dust had been disturbed by long scrapes as though somebody had been dragged unwillingly across it.

Hurrying on this trail he came to a gulch and found that many horses had been there. He tried to count them but he was too excited for accurate tracking.

Disaster had come to the Marlow ranch and that was all that Gilhooly could register.

He whistled excitedly for Calico and the pony came, tripping on his reins. Gilhooly mounted with a rush and spurred around the house. He caught up his lance as he passed it and then swerved back to catch the other trail.

One horse had a notch gone from its shoe and by this mark Gilhooly could follow on the trodden wagon trail.

"It's Fallon," said Gilhooly with the wind in his teeth. "It's that dirty sheepherder Fallon!"

Beyond that he could not go. He accredited Fallon with no great strategy, but only remembered that Mary Ann Marlow was a lovely girl, much in demand but, for some reason which had always been wondrous to Gilhooly, giving most of her time to one Jigs Gilhooly.

And because he had never been able to figure out why she was at all interested in him, he was now more anxious than ever to prove up. And as he rode he pictured what would happen to Fallon.

But Gilhooly completely forgot that he had left his six-gun home because he needed the empty holster for a lance couch. He did not even have his Winchester.

Six men, probably. But the way Gilhooly felt, the six might as well have been six hundred. He balanced his lance and forgot to remember that a rifle bullet can reach a thousand yards with fair accuracy whereas his lance in the same length of time could reach about thirty feet.

He had only read *Ivanhoe* and so he did not know that chivalry had died as the bullet progressed.

Chapter Four

FALLON had a prospector's cabin perched precariously on a hillside above a dry stream bed. Above it five horses filed along the steep trail, picking their careful ways until they reached the flat ground behind the sad shack.

Fallon eased his thick bulk to earth and grinned at Mary Ann. "Now, if you don't mind, young lady, we'll take you in and leave you to sit and think for a spell."

"You'd better watch out!" said Mary Ann, her blue eyes sparking with anger. "If Jigs tracks you to this place, he'll shoot that grin off your face and hang it on the wall."

Fallon appreciated the brave if empty statement. He grinned more broadly. "Yeah? You didn't see what me'n Billings saw last week. Your honey lamb was out pushing a longhorn around with a long stick."

Mary Ann stared down at Fallon. "He was what?"

"You heard me. He's been chewin' on locoweed, sweetheart, and you got as much chance of havin' him pry you out of this with bullets as he has of sayin' no to me now. Now you get inside and be quiet and I'll go over and see if Gilhooly will buy you back."

Mary Ann had never had any real reason to be sure of Gilhooly. He might or might not be dumb and he might or might not be brave. But she wanted very badly to believe that he was bright and brave and so she said that he was in no uncertain terms.

"I tell you that he'll take you apart!" said Mary Ann. "You can't browbeat him into doing anything he doesn't want to do! You want his range so you can get all the range for nothing when the next dry season comes. But Jigs won't give in. Not him! You'd better start leaving the country before he hears about this outrage!"

"Big talk," grinned Fallon, scrubbing his thick jaw and chuckling. "This afternoon I think you'll find out just how brainy and brave this Gilhooly gent is. When he comes here I'll be leadin' him and he'll be as docile as a spring lamb."

Mary Ann wanted to disbelieve that, but she was almost certain it was true. Never in the career of Jigs Gilhooly had anyone said that he was dangerous. And too late she knew that she had accepted his attention to the exclusion of others merely because his company was usually so restful after a hard week's teaching. True, she had wanted him to be romantic but . . .

Fallon hauled her down off the horse, pushed her into the cabin and shut the door.

Stogie and Carson were a little nervous, not liking anything too lawless but not lacking in bravery.

"You sure about this Gilhooly gent?" said Stogie.

"Yeah," said Fallon. "Of course I'm sure." He spat into the dust. "He's big and dumb."

"How about this?" said Carson, jerking his thumb at the cabin.

"Her?" said Fallon. "How about it, Billings?"

Billings grinned. "Aw, by the time the country gets warmed up about this, we'll have Gilhooly's ranch. And as soon as we get that, we get all the money we need. It's been promised."

Stogie and Carson looked a little more convinced and got down.

Fallon turned his horse around and then mounted. "And now, gents, you stay here and keep an eye peeled. I'm going to ride over to Gilhooly's and ask him for his signature. This is too easy."

Fallon spurred his mustang up the trail and over the canyon edge to trot out across the sage-covered plain. He was in a very happy mood as he had never been more certain of anything in his life.

He rode about a mile before he saw the approaching horseman. Once in a while light flashed from bright metal and suddenly Fallon knew that it was Gilhooly.

"Huh," Fallon told himself, "he come right along after all."

Gilhooly was coming, with all the speed that Calico could thunder out of the road. He saw Fallon in the distance and without slackening pace, narrowed the gap to a hundred yards. Then he slowed to a walk and Fallon slowed to a walk and, watchfully, they approached each other.

"Where's Mary Ann?" shouted Gilhooly.

Fallon looked at the tin pail and the long pine stick and chuckled. "She's safe enough. Thanks for ridin' over, Gilhooly. You saved me the trouble of findin' you."

"What for?" said Gilhooly.

"Why, if you will sell your place and water rights, you get back Mary Ann. It's as easy as that."

They were less than a hundred feet apart now, both coming to a halt.

"I got it figured out right," said Gilhooly. "If I sell, you'll block off the wells and the next dry season you can buy the whole range for a song. The ranchers around here would be pretty mad at me, Fallon. It ain't a deal."

"No?" said Fallon. "Well, my boy, it is a deal—but the price is only a thousand dollars now. If you don't sell, I can't promise what'll happen to Mary Ann Marlow."

"You gettin' hard-boiled?" said Gilhooly.

"Yeah," said Fallon.

"Okay, mister," snapped Gilhooly, "you asked for it!"

And before the startled Fallon could so much as blink, Gilhooly quirted Calico and leveled the long lance and charged straight at Fallon.

It was a terrifying thing, to see that spear coming. But Fallon had plenty of time to draw—and draw he did.

He snapped a quick and accurate shot at Gilhooly's thigh and the puncher was almost jerked out of his saddle. But the lance was still in line and still coming.

With a thump the button slammed Fallon in the chest, picked him off his mustang and threw him to earth. The tip struck down, dug sod and before Gilhooly could free it, the pine was snapped in two sections with such force that he too was hurled from his saddle.

He hit rolling and ended up not ten feet from Fallon who was scrambling madly for his lost Colt. Gilhooly dived but he was too late.

Fallon, bruised, blowing and mad, towered above the puncher, Colt leveled. "Funny, ain't you?" snapped Fallon. "I ought to plug you!"

Gilhooly sat still. His thigh was numb and a hole in the batwing told him where the bullet had gone in.

"Ain't so full of ginger now, are you?" said Fallon.

Gilhooly glared through the slits of the water pail and said nothing.

"You changed your mind now?" challenged Fallon.

"What else can I do?" said Gilhooly in a dull voice.

Fallon relaxed a little and grinned. He looked around to see his own pony fleeing for home. Calico was standing by and Fallon approached. Calico shied away but Fallon got the rein.

"You goin' to leave me here?" said Gilhooly on the ground.

"Naw," said Fallon. He mounted and Calico laid back his ears and bucked. But Fallon quirted him into docility and almost broke his jaw with the bit.

"Naw," said Fallon, finishing his sentence, "but I ain't goin' to walk. Come on, puncher. March!"

"But my leg," protested Gilhooly, trying to get up. Then he picked up a five-foot section of the broken lance and pried himself from the earth. Using the pine as a crutch he began to hitch himself along.

"Faster," said Fallon. "I ain't got all day."

Gilhooly hippity-hopped faster, head down.

"This is too easy," said Fallon. "I never did think you had any guts, Gilhooly. We'll go down to my place and sign. But I've cut the price. You don't get but five hundred. I can't pay you less without makin' it suspicious. That all right with you?" he added unnecessarily.

"Yeah," said Gilhooly in a dull voice.

"And after you get paid," said Fallon, "you can leave the country. It won't be healthy for you. Understand?"

Gilhooly didn't answer. He stumped dejectedly along, never turning to look at Fallon.

They came at long last to the rim above the cabin. Gilhooly was played out from loss of blood and the hot sun, and it was all he could do to make it down the trail to the dilapidated shack.

Mary Ann was looking out the window at him and there was both pity and disappointment on her face. But there was no respect.

For her, Gilhooly had passed out of the reach of any respect. He looked so ridiculous with that pail on his head and she judged that his wound would not be serious or else he could not walk at all.

She felt pity and pity is the pallbearer of love.

Fallon got down.

Stogie and Carson and Billings got up from a patch of shade and walked over, gazing amusedly at Gilhooly.

"He tried to get tough, but I took all the fight out of him," said Fallon. "Creased his leg and you'd think he was killed. Ain't that right, Gilhooly?"

Gilhooly looked at the ground through the slits in the pail and said nothing.

"G'wan inside," said Fallon, booting Gilhooly.

Gilhooly walked with difficulty through the door. There was a chair beside the table and he sat down upon it, shoulders slumped in dejection. He would not look up to meet the contempt in Mary Ann's eyes.

Fallon was joyously overbearing. He hauled out some printed forms, some ink and a pen, and shoved them at Gilhooly.

"The more I think about it," said Fallon, "the more I think it would be a shame to spend money on you, Gilhooly. Supposing we make this for ten dollars. Is that all right?" he challenged.

Sorrowfully, Gilhooly nodded. His hand was shaking when he picked up the pen. He dipped it in the ink and tried to make a mark with it.

Stogie and Carson and Billings were standing around grinning.

The pen would not write.

"I got another one," stated Fallon with the air of a man of property. He turned around and rummaged in a box against the far wall.

Gilhooly was still half leaning on his crutch. Stogie and Billings turned to watch Fallon search.

And suddenly the cabin exploded.

Carson saw the stick whip level and he dived for his gun. But before he could draw, hard pine hit him between the eyes and he was slammed sideways against Stogie.

Billings whirled with a warning yell and grabbed at his own gun. *Whack*—and his wrist was broken.

With a backhand on the same sweep, Gilhooly smashed Stogie's nose all over his face.

Fallon roared with anger and leaped up. Gilhooly struck at him but Fallon had time to dodge. The pine stick sailed to crash into the door and drop outside.

Gilhooly and Fallon collided in the middle of the room. Fallon had no time to draw. Gilhooly's fists were too swift. And Fallon's countering blows elicited yells of pain from him. His knuckles were smashed against the improvised casque.

Billings was scrambling for a gun on the floor. Gilhooly leaped up and back and his heels crunched down on Billings' fingers.

Whirling Fallon around with a right, Gilhooly plucked the Colt from its holster and then, reversing its butt, began to get in some work.

The cabin floor was covered with dust that now began to rise chokingly in the room. Through this fog of battle Mary Ann, pressing the far wall with her back, saw a monster with a shining helmet take four men apart with such savage efficiency that it chilled her.

Billings was out of it, a stumbling block on the floor. Stogie could not see for blood and a final crack on the head spilled him into the ashes of the fireplace.

Carson came to and came up fighting. He fired once, but he did not fire twice.

Like a javelin thrower, Gilhooly lanced Carson out through the back window and Carson started an avalanche as he went down the slope.

Gilhooly's helmet had come off in the fray and now, face streaked with sweat and eyes wild with battle, he advanced one final time upon the flailing fists of Fallon.

There was a swift exchange of cracking blows and suddenly Fallon collapsed over Billings. Methodically, Gilhooly reached down and yanked Fallon to his feet only to knock him over again.

"Don't kill him!" screamed Mary Ann.

Gilhooly picked Fallon up and carried him to the water barrel and dumped him in it upside down.

Then he set the bedraggled sheepman in what was left of the chair.

Slowly Fallon came around.

He looked up and saw Gilhooly's set jaw and quailed. "Don't hit me again," pleaded Fallon, fending off.

"You're dumb," stated Gilhooly. "You are the dumbest man I have ever met, in fact."

"How was I to know you wasn't hit?" whined Fallon. "You wasn't square!"

"I'm being square now," said the awful specter of fury which was Gilhooly. "You want my place. Well, I'm going to sell you land, see? I'm going to sell you land and its going to cost you fifteen hundred dollars."

"You'll sell?" gaped Fallon.

Gilhooly snatched the forms to him and grabbed the pen. He scrawled names and locations onto the dotted lines and then signed at the bottom. He reversed the paper and handed the pen.

Fallon read, and what he read he thought must be distorted by his swelling eyes. "But . . . but you're only selling me one acre! You're selling me one acre on the driest part of your land! You can't do this. I won't . . ."

Gilhooly's voice was quiet but Gilhooly's voice went through Fallon's head like a bullet. "Sign and get the money!"

Fallon looked at Gilhooly's face and then Fallon signed. He stumbled over to the box against the back wall and dug out an iron container. Dolefully he counted the contents and found fifteen hundred and forty-five dollars.

Gilhooly snapped it out of his hands. "The forty-five bucks is rent on my horse. Now get out of here. Kick some life into those gents and travel. And don't never come near the Painted Buttes country no more."

He collected the guns and strung them on a piece of wire and went outside to hook them over Calico's horn.

Mary Ann was watching him with wide eyes.

He came back and suddenly he picked her up and carried her out and put her on Carson's sorrel.

The four were collected now. They mounted, watching Gilhooly for any swift move, and then, almost gladly, they rode up the trail and out of sight.

"Oh, Jigs," said Mary Ann, "I never saw anything so wonderful in my life! To fool them into thinking you were wounded and then beating them up and then getting fifteen hundred and forty-five dollars . . ."

"I didn't fool them," said Gilhooly, tenderly regarding his leg. "But say, you know that guy Ivanhoe?"

"Yes, Jigs?"

"He was a fake."

"What?"

"Yeah, why the dickens didn't you tell me that bein' romantic was just beatin' up guys with your bare fists? You'd a saved me a pile of trouble."

Story Preview

Story Preview

NOW that you've just ventured through some of the captivating tales in the Stories from the Golden Age collection by L. Ron Hubbard, turn the page and enjoy a preview of *Branded Outlaw*. Join Lee Weston, who's blamed for rustling cattle. He's almost lynched, but will stop at nothing to find his father's killer . . . until he's framed for shooting the father of the only girl he's ever looked at more than once!

Branded Outlaw

A leather-faced, sun-dried individual with a star on his chest was drowsing over a stack of reward posters, waking up occasionally to swat at a fly which buzzed around his ear. But the instant a shadow appeared in the door, Tate Randall, through long and self-preserving habit, swiftly came to life, one hand half stretched out as a welcoming gesture and the other on the Colt at his side. His bleached eyes squinted as he inspected Lee.

"Say! You're Lee Weston!"

"Right," said Lee.

"Thought you was up in Wyomin' someplace havin' a hell of a time for yourself! Bet old Tom'll be plenty pleased to see you again. Used to stand down by the post office and read us your letters whenever you wrote. I thought—"

"My father was killed last night. The house was burned and the stock run off. I'm giving it to you straight, Randall. I'm looking for Harvey Dodge."

"Huh? Why, man, you must be loco! Harvey Dodge came in and bought the biggest spread in the valley. He's probably the biggest rancher in these parts now. *He* wouldn't do nothin' like that!"

"I'm still looking for Harvey Dodge."

Tate Randall stood up and shook his head. "Sonny, I've

burned enough powder to run a war, and I've shot enough lead to sink a flatboat. If I had it to do over again, I'd use my head and let the law do the findin' and shootin'. If you go gunnin' for Dodge without any more evidence than you've got, there's only one thing that'll happen to you. We'll be building a scaffold out here to string you up. Now think it over. You'n me can ride out and look over this killin' and then—"

In disgust, Lee, turning, started toward the door. But it was blocked by a smooth-shaven, rotund gentleman in a frock coat. Lee saw eyes and hands and thought, "Gambler!"

"What's up, Tate?"

"Doherty, like to have you meet Lee Weston, old Tom's boy."

Ace Doherty extended a be-diamonded hand, which Lee took doubtfully.

"Doherty," continued Tate Randall, "this young feller is about to go on the gun trail for Harvey Dodge. You can back me up that Harvey ain't in town."

"No, he's not around," said Doherty dutifully. "You've got Dodge wrong, youngster. He wouldn't pull any gun tricks, like killin' your old man."

"I don't recall telling you that my father was dead," said Lee.

"Heard it at the store," replied Doherty. "Well, cool him off, Tate. You're the law and order in these parts." He walked away.

Lee faced Randall again. "It's all right to try to cut me down to size, but there's only one thing that counts with me right now, Randall. Last night about twenty men jumped my father. He wrote me his only enemy here was this Harvey Dodge. I'm talking to Dodge."

"Well," shrugged Randall, "if you don't trust justice, you don't trust it, that's all. Trouble with you gunslingers—"

"I don't happen to *be* a gunslinger."

Randall grinned thinly, looking at the well-worn Colts on the younger man's thighs. "Maybe I heard different."

"Maybe you did," said Lee. "But in Wyoming, it hasn't been fixed yet that courts and sheriffs can be used by crooks."

"Maybe you'd better take that back, son."

"I'll reserve judgment on that. But everybody is taking this too calm. The whole town has known for hours what happened out on the Lightning W, and you're still sitting here!"

He ignored the sudden challenge in the old gunfighter's eyes and turned his back upon him to stride out into the hot sunlight. The first thing he noticed was that the street was deserted, even to the loafers on the porch of the general store. He tensed, seeing that a puncher had just led a favored bronc well out of harm's way.

Lee's steps were measured as he approached his buckskin. But things were far from right. He felt a cold chill course down his spine, and turned to face the porch of the Silver Streak Saloon. A thickset man was standing there, arms hanging loosely level with his gun butts. He was unshaven and dirty, but for all that, there was an air of authority about him.

"You lookin' for Dodge, fella?"

Lee came to a stop. "Got anything to offer?"

"Yeah," drawled the man on the porch.

And then it happened. Like a snake striking, the fellow's hands grabbed guns. Lee leaped to the right, flipping his

Colts free. Thunder roared from the porch, and then Lee hammered lead through the pall of smoke which drifted between them.

A pair of boots dropped into sight under the white cloud. Slowly the gunman sagged to the earth, both hands clutched across his stomach, still holding his guns. He made one last effort to fire, but the shot ploughed dust. He lay still.

Lee saw doors swing wide on the other side of the street. Three punchers leaped forth, taking one startled glance at the dead man and then grabbing for their guns.

Across the way, another door opened, to show the muzzle of a Winchester. Lee saw that he had too many on too many sides. He jammed his toe into the buckskin's stirrup and swung over. Shots crashed and a slug almost ripped him from the saddle. Another struck, and his leg went numb.

Valiantly he fired toward the punchers, making them duck for an instant. He dug spur and sped down the street, the Winchester making the air crackle above his head.

Hanging grimly to his horn, his face white with strain, he guided the running buckskin out into the prairie and then north, toward the hill that loomed blue in the distance.

Lee knew that he had only started. The man on the Silver Streak porch had been too young to be Harvey Dodge. He knew that he had just started, but with his life pouring redly from two wounds, he knew that the chances were high against his ever finishing anything but living.

To find out more about *Branded Outlaw* and how you can obtain your copy, go to www.goldenagestories.com.

Glossary

Glossary

STORIES FROM THE GOLDEN AGE *reflect the words and expressions used in the 1930s and 1940s, adding unique flavor and authenticity to the tales. While a character's speech may often reflect regional origins, it also can convey attitudes common in the day. So that readers can better grasp such cultural and historical terms, uncommon words or expressions of the era, the following glossary has been provided.*

---

aces up: in high favor or esteem; first rate, fine or outstanding in some way. In some card games, the ace is the highest valued playing card and "aces up" alludes to the fact that the card player has aces in his hand (the cards dealt to or held by each player) and thus a very good chance of winning.

batwing: one of a pair of batwings; long chaps (leggings worn for protection) with big flaps of leather. They usually fasten with rings and snaps.

Bois-Guilbert, Brian du: Brian de Bois-Guilbert, a knight and the villain in the novel *Ivanhoe*. He and Ivanhoe are mortal enemies.

box: the stagecoach driver's seat.

buffalo robe: the prepared skin of an American bison, with the hair left on, used as a lap robe, rug or blanket.

casque: an open, conical helmet with a nose guard, commonly used in the medieval period.

chinking: on a log cabin, the sticks or rocks used to fill the chink (space between the logs).

clapboard: a type of siding covering the outer walls of buildings in which one edge of each long thin board is thicker than the other. The thick edge of each board overlaps the thin edge of the board below it.

Colt: a single-action, six-shot cylinder revolver, most commonly available in .45- or .44-caliber versions. It was first manufactured in 1873 for the Army by the Colt Firearms Company, the armory founded by American inventor Samuel Colt (1814–1862) who revolutionized the firearms industry with the invention of the revolver. The Colt, also known as the Peacemaker, was also made available to civilians. As a reliable, inexpensive and popular handgun among cowboys, it became known as the "cowboy's gun" and a symbol of the Old West.

Concord: manufactured in Concord, New Hampshire, the one-ton "Concord Coach" was the finest road vehicle of its time, costing $1,050. The wheels were made to withstand the heat and cold. The body was strengthened with iron bands and rested on three-inch-thick oxen-leather braces, installed to prevent injury to the horses that were more valuable to the stage line than any passenger. The interior was four feet wide by four and a half feet high, with adjustable leather curtains, and three padded leather seats (known to be harder than the wood beneath them) for nine passengers. The body was so strong that as many as ten or twelve passengers could perch on top. These stages were beautifully colored, red with yellow trim and gold-leaf scrollwork. However, with all of this, long rides were so uncomfortable that they were known to be "cruel and unusual punishment."

cotillion: a brisk, lively dance characterized by many intricate steps and the continual changing of partners. Used figuratively.

couch: a pocket of sorts for placing or holding a spear or the like in a level position and pointed forward, ready for use.

coyote: a contemptible person, especially a greedy or dishonest one.

dadblamed: confounded; damned.

double-deck: a version of the card game blackjack, played with two decks of cards. Used as a nickname.

drop on, got the: aimed and ready to shoot a gun at an antagonist before the other person's gun can be drawn.

false-front: describes a façade falsifying the size, finish or importance of a building.

flower, in: the finest or most flourishing period.

forked leather: mounted a saddled horse.

forty-four or **.44:** a .44-caliber rifle.

G-men: government men; agents of the Federal Bureau of Investigation.

gone to glory: gone off; lost.

hard-boiled: tough; unsentimental.

hearse plume: on antique horse-drawn hearses, a feather plume, usually ostrich feathers dyed black, used to decorate the tops of the horses' heads.

Ivanhoe: a novel (1819) by Sir Walter Scott (1771–1832), a Scottish novelist and poet who was one of the most prominent figures in English Romanticism.

jack: money.

jigsawing: puzzling; exercising one's mind over some problem or matter.

John B.: Stetson; as the most popular broad-brimmed hat in the West, it became the generic name for *hat*. John B. Stetson was a master hat maker and founder of the company that has been making Stetsons since 1865. Not only can the Stetson stand up to a terrific amount of beating, the cowboy's hat has more different uses than any other garment he wears. It keeps the sun out of the eyes and off the neck; it serves as an umbrella; it makes a great fan, which sometimes is needed when building a fire or shunting cattle about; the brim serves as a cup to water oneself, or as a bucket to water the horse or put out the fire.

lariat: a long noosed rope used for catching horses, cattle, etc.; lasso.

livery stable: a stable that accommodates and looks after horses for their owners.

lobo: wolf; one who is regarded as predatory, greedy and fierce.

locoweed: any of a number of plants widespread in the mountains of the Western US that make livestock act crazy when they eat them.

longhorn: a name given the early cattle of Texas because of the enormous spread of their horns that served for attack and defense. They were not only mean, but the slightest provocation, especially with a bull, would turn them into an aggressive and dangerous enemy. They had lanky bodies and long legs built for speed. A century or so of running wild had made the longhorns tough and hardy enough to withstand blizzards, droughts, dust storms and attacks by other animals and Indians. It took a good horse with a good rider to outrun a longhorn.

neck-reined: guided a horse by pressure of the reins against its neck.

nigh: the left side (of an animal).

plug: a flat cake of pressed or twisted tobacco; chewing tobacco.

polecat: skunk; a thoroughly contemptible person.

puncher: a hired hand who tends cattle and performs other duties on horseback.

quarter: mercy or indulgence, especially as shown in sparing a life and accepting the surrender of a vanquished enemy.

quirted: lashed with a quirt, a flexible, woven-leather whip with a short stock about a foot long.

right-of-way: the right to build and operate a railway line on land belonging to another, or the land so used.

rimfire saddle: a saddle with one cinch that is placed far to the front; also called a *Spanish rig* or *rimmy.*

road agent: stagecoach robber in the mid- to late-nineteenth-century American West.

Scheherazade: the female narrator of *The Arabian Nights,* who during one thousand and one adventurous nights saved her life by entertaining her husband, the king, with stories.

Sharps: any of several models of firearms devised by Christian Sharps and produced by the Sharps Rifle Company until 1881. The most popular Sharps were "Old Reliable," the cavalry carbine, and the heavy-caliber, single-shot buffalo-hunting rifle. Because of its low muzzle velocity, this gun was said to "fire today, kill tomorrow."

slick as a whistle: quickly; easily.

sorrel: a horse with a reddish-brown coat.

tidy: a small covering, usually ornamental, placed on the backs and arms of upholstered furniture to prevent wear or soiling.

tilt course: the tournament grounds on which knights rush at or charge one another, as in a joust.

tinhorn: someone, especially a gambler, who pretends to be important, but actually has little money, influence or skill.

truck farms: farms growing produce for sale commercially; farms producing truck (vegetables raised for the market).

two bits: a quarter; during the colonial days, people used coins from all over the world. When the US adopted an official currency, the Spanish milled (machine-struck) dollar was chosen and it later became the model for American silver dollars. Milled dollars were easily cut apart into equal "bits" of eight pieces. Two bits would equal a quarter of a dollar.

vigilantes: citizens banded together in the West as vigilance committees, without legal sanction and usually in the absence of effective law enforcement, to take action against men viewed as threats to life and property. The usual pattern of vigilance committees was to grab their enemies (guilty or not), stage a sort of trial and hang them. Their other enemies were then likely to get out of town.

Winchester: an early family of repeating rifles; a single-barreled rifle containing multiple rounds of ammunition. Manufactured by the Winchester Repeating Arms Company, it was widely used in the US during the latter half of the nineteenth century. The 1873 model is often called "the gun that won the West" for its immense popularity at that time, as well as its use in fictional Westerns.

yaller pup: yellow dog; a cowardly, despicable person.

ye: the.

L. Ron Hubbard
in the Golden Age
of Pulp Fiction

*In writing an adventure story
a writer has to know that he is adventuring
for a lot of people who cannot.
The writer has to take them here and there
about the globe and show them
excitement and love and realism.
As long as that writer is living the part of an
adventurer when he is hammering
the keys, he is succeeding with his story.*

*Adventuring is a state of mind.
If you adventure through life, you have a
good chance to be a success on paper.*

*Adventure doesn't mean globe-trotting,
exactly, and it doesn't mean great deeds.
Adventuring is like art.
You have to live it to make it real.*

— *L. RON HUBBARD*

L. Ron Hubbard
and American
Pulp Fiction

B ORN March 13, 1911, L. Ron Hubbard lived a life at least as expansive as the stories with which he enthralled a hundred million readers through a fifty-year career.

Originally hailing from Tilden, Nebraska, he spent his formative years in a classically rugged Montana, replete with the cowpunchers, lawmen and desperadoes who would later people his Wild West adventures. And lest anyone imagine those adventures were drawn from vicarious experience, he was not only breaking broncs at a tender age, he was also among the few whites ever admitted into Blackfoot society as a bona fide blood brother. While if only to round out an otherwise rough and tumble youth, his mother was that rarity of her time—a thoroughly educated woman—who introduced her son to the classics of Occidental literature even before his seventh birthday.

But as any dedicated L. Ron Hubbard reader will attest, his world extended far beyond Montana. In point of fact, and as the son of a United States naval officer, by the age of eighteen he had traveled over a quarter of a million miles. Included therein were three Pacific crossings to a then still mysterious Asia, where he ran with the likes of Her British Majesty's agent-in-place

L. Ron Hubbard, left, at Congressional Airport, Washington, DC, 1931, with members of George Washington University flying club.

for North China, and the last in the line of Royal Magicians from the court of Kublai Khan. For the record, L. Ron Hubbard was also among the first Westerners to gain admittance to forbidden Tibetan monasteries below Manchuria, and his photographs of China's Great Wall long graced American geography texts.

Upon his return to the United States and a hasty completion of his interrupted high school education, the young Ron Hubbard entered George Washington University. There, as fans of his aerial adventures may have heard, he earned his wings as a pioneering barnstormer at the dawn of American aviation. He also earned a place in free-flight record books for the longest sustained flight above Chicago. Moreover, as a roving reporter for *Sportsman Pilot* (featuring his first professionally penned articles), he further helped inspire a generation of pilots who would take America to world airpower.

Immediately beyond his sophomore year, Ron embarked on the first of his famed ethnological expeditions, initially to then untrammeled Caribbean shores (descriptions of which would later fill a whole series of West Indies mystery-thrillers). That the Puerto Rican interior would also figure into the future of Ron Hubbard stories was likewise no accident. For in addition to cultural studies of the island, a 1932–33

LRH expedition is rightly remembered as conducting the first complete mineralogical survey of a Puerto Rico under United States jurisdiction.

There was many another adventure along this vein: As a lifetime member of the famed Explorers Club, L. Ron Hubbard charted North Pacific waters with the first shipboard radio direction finder, and so pioneered a long-range navigation system universally employed until the late twentieth century. While not to put too fine an edge on it, he also held a rare Master Mariner's license to pilot any vessel, of any tonnage in any ocean.

Yet lest we stray too far afield, there is an LRH note at this juncture in his saga, and it reads in part:

"I started out writing for the pulps, writing the best I knew, writing for every mag on the stands, slanting as well as I could."

To which one might add: His earliest submissions date from the summer of 1934, and included tales drawn from true-to-life Asian adventures, with characters roughly modeled on British/American intelligence operatives he had known in Shanghai. His early Westerns were similarly peppered with details drawn from personal experience. Although therein lay a first hard lesson from the often cruel world of the pulps. His first Westerns were soundly rejected as lacking the authenticity of a Max Brand yarn

Capt. L. Ron Hubbard in Ketchikan, Alaska, 1940, on his Alaskan Radio Experimental Expedition, the first of three voyages conducted under the Explorers Club flag.

(a particularly frustrating comment given L. Ron Hubbard's Westerns came straight from his Montana homeland, while Max Brand was a mediocre New York poet named Frederick Schiller Faust, who turned out implausible six-shooter tales from the terrace of an Italian villa).

Nevertheless, and needless to say, L. Ron Hubbard persevered and soon earned a reputation as among the most publishable names in pulp fiction, with a ninety percent placement rate of first-draft manuscripts. He was also among the most prolific, averaging between seventy and a hundred thousand words a month. Hence the rumors that L. Ron Hubbard had redesigned a typewriter for faster keyboard action and pounded out manuscripts on a continuous roll of butcher paper to save the precious seconds it took to insert a single sheet of paper into manual typewriters of the day.

That all L. Ron Hubbard stories did not run beneath said byline is yet another aspect of pulp fiction lore. That is, as publishers periodically rejected manuscripts from top-drawer authors if only to avoid paying top dollar, L. Ron Hubbard and company just as frequently replied with submissions under various pseudonyms. In Ron's case, the list

A MAN OF MANY NAMES

Between 1934 and 1950, L. Ron Hubbard authored more than fifteen million words of fiction in more than two hundred classic publications. To supply his fans and editors with stories across an array of genres and pulp titles, he adopted fifteen pseudonyms in addition to his already renowned L. Ron Hubbard byline.

Winchester Remington Colt
Lt. Jonathan Daly
Capt. Charles Gordon
Capt. L. Ron Hubbard
Bernard Hubbel
Michael Keith
Rene Lafayette
Legionnaire 148
Legionnaire 14830
Ken Martin
Scott Morgan
Lt. Scott Morgan
Kurt von Rachen
Barry Randolph
Capt. Humbert Reynolds

110

included: Rene Lafayette, Captain Charles Gordon, Lt. Scott Morgan and the notorious Kurt von Rachen—supposedly on the lam for a murder rap, while hammering out two-fisted prose in Argentina. The point: While L. Ron Hubbard as Ken Martin spun stories of Southeast Asian intrigue, LRH as Barry Randolph authored tales of romance on the Western range—which, stretching between a dozen genres is how he came to stand among the two hundred elite authors providing close to a million tales through the glory days of American Pulp Fiction.

L. Ron Hubbard, circa 1930, at the outset of a literary career that would finally span half a century.

In evidence of exactly that, by 1936 L. Ron Hubbard was literally leading pulp fiction's elite as president of New York's American Fiction Guild. Members included a veritable pulp hall of fame: Lester "Doc Savage" Dent, Walter "The Shadow" Gibson, and the legendary Dashiell Hammett—to cite but a few.

Also in evidence of just where L. Ron Hubbard stood within his first two years on the American pulp circuit: By the spring of 1937, he was ensconced in Hollywood, adopting a Caribbean thriller for Columbia Pictures, remembered today as *The Secret of Treasure Island.* Comprising fifteen thirty-minute episodes, the L. Ron Hubbard screenplay led to the most profitable matinée serial in Hollywood history. In accord with Hollywood culture, he was thereafter continually called

The 1937 Secret of Treasure Island, *a fifteen-episode serial adapted for the screen by L. Ron Hubbard from his novel,* Murder at Pirate Castle.

upon to rewrite/doctor scripts—most famously for long-time friend and fellow adventurer Clark Gable.

In the interim—and herein lies another distinctive chapter of the L. Ron Hubbard story—he continually worked to open Pulp Kingdom gates to up-and-coming authors. Or, for that matter, anyone who wished to write. It was a fairly unconventional stance, as markets were already thin and competition razor sharp. But the fact remains, it was an L. Ron Hubbard hallmark that he vehemently lobbied on behalf of young authors—regularly supplying instructional articles to trade journals, guest-lecturing to short story classes at George Washington University and Harvard, and even founding his own creative writing competition. It was established in 1940, dubbed the Golden Pen, and guaranteed winners both New York representation and publication in *Argosy*.

But it was John W. Campbell Jr.'s *Astounding Science Fiction* that finally proved the most memorable LRH vehicle. While every fan of L. Ron Hubbard's galactic epics undoubtedly knows the story, it nonetheless bears repeating: By late 1938, the pulp publishing magnate of Street & Smith was determined to revamp *Astounding Science Fiction* for broader readership. In particular, senior editorial director F. Orlin Tremaine called for stories with a stronger *human element*. When acting editor John W. Campbell balked, preferring his spaceship-driven tales,

Tremaine enlisted Hubbard. Hubbard, in turn, replied with the genre's first truly *character-driven* works, wherein heroes are pitted not against bug-eyed monsters but the mystery and majesty of deep space itself—and thus was launched the Golden Age of Science Fiction.

The names alone are enough to quicken the pulse of any science fiction aficionado, including LRH friend and protégé, Robert Heinlein, Isaac Asimov, A. E. van Vogt and Ray Bradbury. Moreover, when coupled with LRH stories of fantasy, we further come to what's rightly been described as the foundation of every modern tale of horror: L. Ron Hubbard's immortal Fear. It was rightly proclaimed by Stephen King as one of the very few works to genuinely warrant that overworked term "classic"—as in: *"This is a classic tale of creeping, surreal menace and horror. . . . This is one of the really, really good ones."*

L. Ron Hubbard, 1948, among fellow science fiction luminaries at the World Science Fiction Convention in Toronto.

To accommodate the greater body of L. Ron Hubbard fantasies, Street & Smith inaugurated *Unknown*—a classic pulp if there ever was one, and wherein readers were soon thrilling to the likes of *Typewriter in the Sky* and *Slaves of Sleep* of which Frederik Pohl would declare: *"There are bits and pieces from Ron's work that became part of the language in ways that very few other writers managed."*

And, indeed, at J. W. Campbell Jr.'s insistence, Ron was regularly drawing on themes from the Arabian Nights and so introducing readers to a world of genies, jinn, Aladdin and Sinbad—all of which, of course, continue to float through cultural mythology to this day.

At least as influential in terms of post-apocalypse stories was L. Ron Hubbard's 1940 *Final Blackout*. Generally acclaimed as the finest anti-war novel of the decade and among the ten best works of the genre ever authored—here, too, was a tale that would live on in ways few other writers

imagined. Hence, the later Robert Heinlein verdict: "Final Blackout *is as perfect a piece of science fiction as has ever been written.*"

Like many another who both lived and wrote American pulp adventure, the war proved a tragic end to Ron's sojourn in the pulps. He served with distinction in four theaters and was highly decorated

Portland, Oregon, 1943; L. Ron Hubbard captain of the US Navy subchaser PC 815.

for commanding corvettes in the North Pacific. He was also grievously wounded in combat, lost many a close friend and colleague and thus resolved to say farewell to pulp fiction and devote himself to what it had supported these many years—namely, his serious research.

But in no way was the LRH literary saga at an end, for as he wrote some thirty years later, in 1980:

"Recently there came a period when I had little to do. This was novel in a life so crammed with busy years, and I decided to amuse myself by writing a novel that was pure science fiction."

That work was *Battlefield Earth: A Saga of the Year 3000*. It was an immediate *New York Times* bestseller and, in fact, the first international science fiction blockbuster in decades. It was not, however, L. Ron Hubbard's magnum opus, as that distinction is generally reserved for his next and final work: The 1.2 million word *Mission Earth*.

> **Final Blackout**
> *is as perfect a piece of science fiction as has ever been written.*
>
> —Robert Heinlein

How he managed those 1.2 million words in just over twelve months is yet another piece of the L. Ron Hubbard legend. But the fact remains, he did indeed author a ten-volume *dekalogy* that lives in publishing history for the fact that each and every volume of the series was also a *New York Times* bestseller.

Moreover, as subsequent generations discovered L. Ron Hubbard through republished works and novelizations of his screenplays, the mere fact of his name on a cover signaled an international bestseller. . . . Until, to date, sales of his works exceed hundreds of millions, and he otherwise remains among the most enduring and widely read authors in literary history. Although as a final word on the tales of L. Ron Hubbard, perhaps it's enough to simply reiterate what editors told readers in the glory days of American Pulp Fiction:

He writes the way he does, brothers, because he's been there, seen it and done it!

115

THE STORIES FROM THE GOLDEN AGE

Your ticket to adventure starts here with the Stories from
the Golden Age collection by master storyteller L. Ron Hubbard.
These gripping tales are set in a kaleidoscope of exotic locales and brim
with fascinating characters, including some of the
most vile villains, dangerous dames and brazen heroes
you'll ever get to meet.

The entire collection of over one hundred and fifty stories is being
released in a series of eighty books and audiobooks.
For an up-to-date listing of available titles,
go to www.goldenagestories.com.

AIR ADVENTURE

FAR-FLUNG ADVENTURE

SEA ADVENTURE

TALES FROM THE ORIENT

The Devil—With Wings   *Pearl Pirate*
The Falcon Killer   *The Red Dragon*
Five Mex for a Million   *Spy Killer*
Golden Hell   *Tah*
The Green God   *The Trail of the Red Diamonds*
Hurricane's Roar   *Wind-Gone-Mad*
Inky Odds   *Yellow Loot*
Orders Is Orders

MYSTERY

The Blow Torch Murder   *The Grease Spot*
Brass Keys to Murder   *Killer Ape*
Calling Squad Cars!   *Killer's Law*
The Carnival of Death   *The Mad Dog Murder*
The Chee-Chalker   *Mouthpiece*
Dead Men Kill   *Murder Afloat*
The Death Flyer   *The Slickers*
Flame City   *They Killed Him Dead*

119

FANTASY

Borrowed Glory	*If I Were You*
The Crossroads	*The Last Drop*
Danger in the Dark	*The Room*
The Devil's Rescue	*The Tramp*
He Didn't Like Cats	

SCIENCE FICTION

The Automagic Horse	*A Matter of Matter*
Battle of Wizards	*The Obsolete Weapon*
Battling Bolto	*One Was Stubborn*
The Beast	*The Planet Makers*
Beyond All Weapons	*The Professor Was a Thief*
A Can of Vacuum	*The Slaver*
The Conroy Diary	*Space Can*
The Dangerous Dimension	*Strain*
Final Enemy	*Tough Old Man*
The Great Secret	*240,000 Miles Straight Up*
Greed	*When Shadows Fall*
The Invaders	

WESTERN

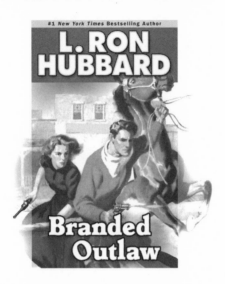

JOIN THE PULP REVIVAL
America in the 1930s and 40s

Pulp fiction was in its heyday and 30 million readers were regularly riveted by the larger-than-life tales of master storyteller L. Ron Hubbard. For this was pulp fiction's golden age, when the writing was raw and every page packed a walloping punch.

That magic can now be yours. An evocative world of nefarious villains, exotic intrigues, courageous heroes and heroines—a world that today's cinema has barely tapped for tales of adventure and swashbucklers.

Enroll today in the Stories from the Golden Age Club and begin receiving your monthly feature edition selected from more than 150 stories in the collection.

You may choose to enjoy them as either a paperback or audiobook for the special membership price of $9.95 each month along with FREE shipping and handling.

CALL TOLL-FREE: 1-877-8GALAXY
(1-877-842-5299) OR GO ONLINE TO
www.goldenagestories.com
AND BECOME PART OF THE PULP REVIVAL!

Prices are set in US dollars only. For non-US residents, please call
1-323-466-7815 for pricing information. Free shipping available for US residents only.

Galaxy Press, 7051 Hollywood Blvd., Suite 200, Hollywood, CA 90028